Janet Edmondson Walker

Fortune by Land and Sea

A Tragi-comedy

Janet Edmondson Walker

Fortune by Land and Sea
A Tragi-comedy

ISBN/EAN: 9783744788458

Printed in Europe, USA, Canada, Australia, Japan

Cover: Foto ©Andreas Hilbeck / pixelio.de

More available books at **www.hansebooks.com**

Fortune by Land and Sea

A Tragi-Comedy

BY

Thomas Heywood

AND

William Rowley

Acting Version arranged for the Annual Theatricals of the Harvard Chapter of Delta Upsilon for 1899

BY

Janet Edmondson Walker

Together with brief sketches of Thomas Heywood, Philip Henslow, and other notes of interest

Also a reprint of the full text of the play

W. B. CLARKE COMPANY
PARK STREET CHURCH
BOSTON, MASSACHUSETTS, U.S.A.
1899

TO THE
HARVARD CHAPTER OF THE DELTA UPSILON FRATERNITY
THIS BOOK IS RESPECTFULLY DEDICATED

PREFACE.

It was with the greatest reverence that I approached the task of reconstructing Thomas Heywood's play for modern stage production. Any variation from the original, either in the arrangement of scenes or in omissions, has been made with a view to bringing out the dramatic value of the work, and placing before the public the story of the play in a connected form, that its picturesque beauties may be more quickly grasped and appreciated.

Sometimes a word or sentence has been changed after a careful study of the context, where the meaning was vague or the word obsolete. The opening of Scene 2, Act I., has been introduced from Heywood's "Fair Maid of the West," in order to give a more vivid picture of tavern life of the time. As such innovations were frequent during the Elizabethan period, it cannot be taken amiss to follow the example of those dramatists, and add a touch of color to the scene in Heywood's own words.

The stage directions are my own, as the edition from which I prepared my acting version gave none. These have been suggested either by the text or a study of the manners and customs of those days. In all things I have tried to keep in mind what Heywood would himself have done with the players at the " Rose " or " Fortune " theatre where he acted. We know on good authority that this play was not published until after its author's death. We also know from Kirkman that many of Heywood's plays "were written in taverns on the backside of tavern bills." This may account for the vagueness of certain passages, as such manuscripts must have been very fragmentary; or it may be that what has come down to us was one of the copies which Heywood complained of as "corrupt and mangled, copied only out of the ear." Considering all these facts, it cannot be deemed an undue liberty to endeavor by a little respectful editing to make the author's meaning clear.

In speaking of one of Heywood's plays that was very popular, it being represented before James I. and his queen three times in the space of eight days, John Addington Symonds quotes the following from a writer of that time: "It was produced under the wise conduct of that admirable artist, Mr. Inigo Jones, master-surveyor of the King's work, etc., who to every act, nay, almost to every scene, by his excellent inventions gave such an extraordinary lustre — *upon every occasion changing the stage*, to the admiration of all the spectators — that as I most ingenuously confess, it was above my apprehension to conceive." This account, it seems to me, would be sufficient authority to justify the use of scenery in any revival of the Elizabethan drama, instead of clinging to the traditional rushes and tallow dips.

In publishing the full text of the play, in order that the reader may compare it with my acting version, I have chosen Barron Field's edition, as that is the one more familiar to students.

JANET EDMONDSON WALKER.

BOSTON, February, 1899.

THOMAS HEYWOOD.

I DO not know whether Thomas Heywood ever had permission from the Crown to write "Gentleman" after his name, or whether he could so style himself by right of inheritance; but certain it is that he was so accounted in the hearts of his friends and contemporaries, and deserved the title in its broadest, truest sense. "He was a fellow actor and fellow dramatist with Shakspeare," says Charles Lamb. "He possessed not the imagination of the latter, but in all those qualities which gained for Shakspeare the attribute of gentle, he was not inferior to him — generosity, courtesy, temperance in the depths of passion; sweetness, in a word, and gentleness." In speaking of Heywood's work, Mr. Symonds says: "His means of reaching the heart are of the simplest. He depends for his tragic effects upon no Até, no midnight horrors, no sarcastic knave. Yet his use of some name, '*Nan, Nan*,' and his allusions to Christ and our religion, go straight to the very soul."

His men are all gentlemen, but he seems to have taken special delight in portraying brave, high-spirited young men. "Nothing could be finer," to again quote Mr. Symonds, "than the bearing of Young Forrest (in Fortune by Land and Sea) when he challenges Rainsforth."

Little seems to be known or rather recorded about the birth and family of Heywood beyond the fact that he was a native of Lincolnshire, but I should judge that he belonged to the upper middle class. That he was a man of fine literary taste is shown by the character of his miscellaneous writings, and he was a versatile as well as a prolific writer. Besides having had a hand in over two hundred and twenty dramas, he wrote the Lord Mayor's pageants for many years, and various prologues and eulogies. He also delighted in the labor of compilation, and had for some time on hand a Biographical Dictionary of all the poets, from the most remote period of the world's history down to his own time. What he accomplished in his profession outside of literature was quite remarkable. We are told by Kirkman that "he acted every day," and was a member of the Lord Admiral's, Earl of Southampton's, Earl of Derby's, Earl of Worcester's, and the Queen's companies. After the death of the Queen in 1603, he went back to the Earl of Worcester's company, but before that we hear of him in 1594 as an actor and author under the management of Philip Henslow. During this period Heywood must have acted at the " Rose " theatre, it being the only one Henslow owned at that time. I can find no record of the time or place of Heywood's death, except that he lived to a ripe old age and died in the middle of the 17th century.

There were four other dramatic poets named Heywood.

John Heywood (1500–1580). "A sort of Court Jester, though of good social position, who amused by his powers of repartee. Author of a popular work, "Epigrams and Proverbs," besides several plays. He wrote three interludes in which for the first time characters were personal and not mere abstractions, and thus paved the way for English Comedy."— *Century Cyclopædia*.

Elizæus. " Eldest son of John Heywood, published his ' Il Moro,' dedicated to Cardinal Pole, in 1556. Joined the society of Jesus in 1562."— *Biog. Drama*.

Jasper. "Second son of John Heywood, was born 1535. He was translator of three tragedies attributed to Seneca: 'Thyestes,' 1561; 'Hercules Furens,' 1561; 'Troas,' 1581. Became a priest, and subsequently provincial of the Society of Jesus. He was treated with severity in the Tower and ultimately banished in 1585."—*Biog. Drama*.

Matthew Heywood. "Author of a comedy called the 'Changeling.'

" Matthew and Thomas Heywood were not relatives, neither were they related to John Heywood."—*John Green's " Odds and Ends " of Covent Garden and the ancient drama, compiled from various manuscripts and published in London in the early part of the present century.*

J. E. W.

PHILIP HENSLOW.

(UNDER WHOSE MANAGEMENT THOMAS HEYWOOD ACTED AND WROTE PLAYS.)

———————

PHILIP HENSLOW was one of those persons who, dull in themselves, do the greatest service to literature by jotting down trifling de-
tails of the life going on about them, thus giving us in a few words
a vivid picture of the men and manners of the time. He began life
as servant or clerk to the bailiff of Viscount Montague, having
charge of the Viscount's town house in Southwark, a parliamentary
borough of London situated on the southern bank of the Thames.
Henslow's diary tells us that he loaned money to actors or advanced
it upon their plays. He also bought the manuscripts of dramas, pay-
ing sums like eight and ten pounds for a play. This investment of
his savings while bailiff's clerk must have proved a successful venture for Henslow, as at that time the drama was in the height of
popularity, patronized by Royalty, whose seal of approval set the
fashion of the day. At all events, we read that Henslow "gradually
made money and bought property." He owned several inns, one of
which, the Boar's Head tavern, was made famous by Shakspeare as
the scene of Falstaff's carousals. In 1585, Henslow bought land
at Bankside, a small district lying on the south side of the Thames
between Blackfriars and Waterloo bridges. Bankside belonged to
the manor of Southwark and, not being included in the grant to the
City, it virtually enjoyed the privilege of asylum like Blackfriars, its
neighbor on the opposite side of the river. Players had been ex-
pelled from the city limits, but the Sheriff could not touch them here.
 In this quaint old quarter, under the shadow of the church of
St. Mary Avaries, and not far from the grim walls of the Clink
prison, wise Philip Henslow built in 1592 the "Rose Theatre." It
is an interesting fact to note that Henslow's Rose theatre was built
four years previous to the erection of the Blackfriars theatre, which
has been generally spoken of as the first theatre in London. Several entries in Henslow's diary alluding to the cost of "theatrical
wardrobe for the Blackfriars" have led some writers to assume that
he had an interest in the playhouse associated with Shakspeare's

name, but he evidently meant his own house, "the Fortune," and the mistake presumably arose from confusing the Blackfriars theatre with the locality of the same name.

As a theatrical manager, Henslow was quite as successful as he had been as a money lender and inn-keeper, for in 1599 the management of the Blackfriars theatre (built in 1596) sought to share his patronage by building a rival theatre in Bankside, called the "Globe." Henslow returned the compliment in the following year (1600) by erecting in Blackfriars a fine theatre, "The Fortune." In this enterprise he had the co-operation of Alleyn, reckoned one of the best actors of his day and afterwards founder of Dulwich College. Henslow was a good business man, saving and thrifty, and ought to have left a fine fortune behind him. If he did so, I can find no record of who profited by his wealth after his death in 1616.

J. E. W.

BARRON FIELD (1789-1846).

"BARRON FIELD, lawyer and misc. writer, 2d son of Henry Field, treasurer of Apothecaries Co. by his wife Esther, daughter of John Barron, was born Oct. 23, 1786. Intimate and dear acquaintance of Charles Lamb. Knew Coleridge, Wordsworth, Hazlitt, Leigh Hunt, etc. Early supported himself by literature. Theatrical critic of the *Times*. Appointed official at Ceylon, then Judge of Supreme Court of New S. Wales. Stayed there seven years. (See impressions in London Magazine 1822-5, also 'Geographical Memoirs of New South Wales'). Unjustly (?) charged with encouraging litigation to augment his income. Quick to embark in the party squabbles of the colony. Next appointed to chief-justiceship at Gibraltar, where Benj. Disraeli visited him 1830 and left a disparaging account of his manners. Died childless, April 11, 1846. He edited for the Shakspeare Soc. (1) The First and Second Parts of King Edward IV., Histories by Thos. Heywood, (1842); (2) The True Tragedy of Richard III. (1844); (3) The Fair Maid of the Exchange, by Heywood, and Fortune by Land and Sea, by Heywood & Rowley, (1846). Was always an extravagant admirer of Heywood and had planned to edit all his works, but death prevented."

From Leslie Stephen, Dict. Nat. Biog.

Extract from Barron Field's introduction to "Fortune by Land and Sea" : —

"It would seem unnatural now-a-days that an eldest son for marrying a young lady with no fortune, should by his father be not only disinherited but made together with his wife domestic servants to the father and younger brothers; but in Shakspeare's day such patriarchal tyranny could be practised with no check from public opinion. The land generally went by heirship to the eldest son and younger brothers under pretence of having the run of the house were virtually servants to the heir."

FORTUNE BY LAND AND SEA

A Tragi-Comedy

As it was acted with great applause by
the Queen's servants

Written by

THOMAS HEYWOOD
&
WILLIAM ROWLEY

LONDON

Printed for *John Sweeting* at the *Angel* in
Pope's-head Alley, and *Robert Pollard*, at the
Ben Johnson's Head behind the Exchange
1655

THE PERSONS OF THE PLAY.

OLD FORREST.

FRANK FORREST, } his sons.
YOUNG FORREST,

OLD HARDING.

PHILIP, his eldest son, married to SUSAN FORREST.

WILLIAM, } his younger sons.
JOHN,

MASTER RAINSFORTH, a quarrelsome Gentleman.

GOODWIN, } Friends to Rainsford.
FOSTER,

A MERCHANT, brother to MRS. HARDING.

PURSER, } Pirates.
CLINTON,

CLOWN.

PURSUIVANT.

HOST.

SAILOR.

HANGMAN.

DRAWERS.

OFFICERS.

MRS. ANN HARDING, second wife to OLD HARDING.

SUSAN, daughter of OLD FORREST, wife to PHILIP HARDING.

BESS, barmaid.

The SCENE London.

ACT I.

Scene i.—*A Street.*

Enter L. Old Forrest, Frank Forrest, Susan.
Enter R. Mr. Rainsforth, Goodwin, *and* Foster. *Bow, and, as they pass each other,* Rainsforth *touches* Frank Forrest *on shoulder, detaining him, and speaks low.*

Rainsforth: I prithee, Frank, let's have thy company to supper.

Frank: With all my heart. If I can but give my father here the slip by six o'clock, I will not fail.

Rainsforth: I'll talk with him. (*Crosses to* Old Forrest.) I prithee, old man, lend's thy son to-night. We'll borrow him but some two hours, and send him home again to thee presently.

Goodwin: Faith, do, Mr. Forrest. He cannot spend his time in better company.

Old Forrest: Ah! gentlemen, his too much liberty breeds many strange, outrageous ills in youth, and fashions them to vice.

Rainsforth: Nay, school us not, old man. Some of us are too old to learn; and, being past whipping, too, there's no hope of profiting. If we shall have him, say so. If not, I prithee keep him still, and God give thee good of him.

Frank: Nay, will you be gone? I'll be at the heels of you as I live.

Foster (*to* Rainsforth): 'Tis enough. Let's go.

Old Forrest: Nay, gentlemen, do not mistake me, pray. I love my son, but do not dote on him. Nor is he such a darling in mine eye that I am loath to have him from my sight. Yet let me tell you, had you, gentlemen, called him to any fairer exercise, as practice of known weapons or to back some gallant steed,* had it been to dance, leap in the fields, to wrestle, or to try masteries in any noble quality, I could have spared him to you half his age. But call him out to drinking! Of all skill, I hold that much used practice the most ill.

* Original "gennet," a Spanish horse.— *Skeat.*

RAINSFORTH : Sir, what we do's in love. And let you know, we do not need his purse nor his acquaintance. Nor, if you should take aught amiss, can we be sorry, nor strive * to ask your pardon. Fare you well. Come, gentlemen.

(*Exeunt R.* RAINSFORTH *and* GOODWIN.)

OLD FORREST : Oh, son, that thou wilt follow rioting, surfeit by drinking and unseasoned hours! These gentlemen perhaps may do it, they're rich, well landed, and their fathers purchase daily where I, Heaven knows, the world still frowning on me, am forced to sell and mortgage to keep you. His brother ranks himself with the best gallants that flourish in the kingdom ; is honoured for his great learning, his person wooed and sought by them more bound to him for his discourse, than he to them for their expense and cost. Thy course is otherwise, thee not able to spend with them. Will drinking healths, cups of mulled sack, and glasses elbow deep, drunk in thy youth, maintain thee in thy age ? No, 'twill not hold out, boy.

FRANK : My company hath not been to your purse so chargeable. I do not spend so much.

OLD FORREST : Thou spendest thy time, more precious than thy coin ; consumest thy hopes, thy fortune and thy after expectations in drowning surfeits. Tell me, canst thou call that thrift, to be prodigal in all these. Use thy discretion. Somewhat I divine, mine is the care, the loss or profit thine.

(*Exit L.*)

SUSAN : Brother, be ruled. My father grieves to see you given to these boundless riots. Will you follow ?

FRANK : Lead you the way, I'll after you.

SUSAN : 'Tis well ; he'll look for you within.

(*Exeunt L.*)

SCENE 2.— *Tap-room in Inn.*

At rise of curtain gallants drinking at tables. PURSER *and* CLINTON *seated at table down stage. Song at one of the tables, etc. Enter* MERCHANT *and* CAPTAIN GOODLASH.

1ST DRAWER : You are welcome, gentlemen.

2ND DRAWER : Look out a towel and some rolls, a salt and trenchers.

* Original " wound "; Anglo-Saxon, winnan, strive.—*Skeat.*

MERCHANT: No, sir, we will not dine.

1ST DRAWER: I am sure you would if you had my stomach (*goes up stage*).

2ND DRAWER: What wine drink ye, sack or claret?

MERCHANT: Where's Bess?

2ND DRAWER: Marry, above, with three or four gentlemen.

MERCHANT: Go, call her.

2ND DRAWER: I'll draw you a cup of the neatest wine in London.

MERCHANT: I'll taste none of your drawing, go call Bess (*sits at table*).

2ND DRAWER: There's nothing in the mouths of these gallants but "Bess, Bess."

MERCHANT: What say you, sir?

2ND DRAWER: Nothing, sir; but I'll go call her.

MERCHANT: When put we to sea?

CAPTAIN GOODLASH: When the wind's fair. But pray tell me, why, being a man well revenued, will you adventure thus a doubtful voyage, when only such as I, born to no other fortune, should seek abroad for pillage?

MERCHANT: Pillage, Captain! Nay, 'tis for honour, no hope of gain or spoil, that draws me.

CAPT. G.: Ay, but what draws you to this house so oft?

MERCHANT: As if thou knew'st it not!

CAPT. G.: What, Bess?

MERCHANT: Even she.

CAPT. G.: Come, I must tell you, you forget yourself. One of your birth and breeding thus to dote upon a tanner's daughter! Why, her father sold hides in Somersetshire, and being trade-fallen sent her to service.

MERCHANT: Prithee, speak no more, thou tellest me that which I would fain forget or wish I had not known. If thou wilt humour me, tell me she's fair and honest.

CAPT. G.: Yes, and loves you.

MERCHANT: To forget that were to exclude the rest — See, she comes!

Enter BESS.

BESS: Sweet Master, you're a stranger grown. Where have you been these three days?

MERCHANT: Last night I sat up late at game. Here, take this bag and lay't up till I call for it.

BESS: Sir, I shall.

MERCHANT: Bring some wine.

BESS: I know your taste and I shall please your palate.

(Exit.)

CLINTON: In your time have you seen a sweeter creature? She hath almost undone the other taverns; the gallants make no rendezvous now but at the Castle.

PURSER: Spite of them I shall have her.

CLINTON: Do you think she is so easily won?

PURSER: Easily or not, I'll bid as fair and far as any man within twenty miles of my head.

Enter BESS.

BESS: 'Tis of the best Graves wine, sir.

MERCHANT: Gramercy, girl, come sit.

BESS: Pray pardon, sir, I dare not.

MERCHANT: But I'll have it so.

BESS: My fellow servants love me not and will complain of such a saucy boldness.

CAPT. G.: Out on your fellows! I'll try whether their pottle pots or heads be harder if I do but hear them grumble.

MERCHANT: Sit now, Bess, and drink to me.

BESS (taking mug): To your good voyage — (drinks).

Enter 1ST DRAWER.

1ST DRAWER: Bess, you must fill some wine into the Portcullis. (Aside) Must you be set and we wait?

MERCHANT: What say you, sir?

1ST DRAWER: The gentlemen will drink none but of her drawing.

BESS (rising): Pray pardon, sir, I needs must be gone.

MERCHANT (detaining her): She shall not rise, sir, go, let your master snick up.*

BESS: Pray give me leave to fill for them.

MERCHANT: First one word with you alone.

* Go hang.

BESS (*to* DRAWER): Go, say I come anon. (*Exit* DRAWER). (*To Merchant*) Is aught amiss with thee?

MERCHANT: Bess, all my afflictions are that I must leave thee; thou knowest my necessity.

BESS: Is it coin you want? Here is the hundred pound you gave me late; use that, beside what I have saved and stored, which makes it fifty more. Were it ten thousand, nay, a whole million, all were thine. I wish I had been born equal to you, or you so low to have been ranked with me. I could then have presumed to say I love you.

MERCHANT: Bess, I thank thee. Keep still that hundred pounds till my return. If never, wench, take it; it is thine own. Time calls hence. We now must part.

BESS: Farewell!

MERCHANT: A thousand farewells are in one contracted (*kisses her*). Come, Captain, away.

(*Exit.*)

PURSER (*coming to* BESS): What gentlemen are those?

BESS: Sir, they are such as please to be our guests.

PURSER: Give me their names.

BESS: You may go search the church book where they were christened; there you, perhaps, may learn them.

PURSER: How, minion? (*seizes her roughly.*)

BESS: Pray, hands off!

CLINTON (*separating them*): Fie! fie! you are too rude with this fair creature.

PURSER: I tell thee, maid, no man shall kiss thee but by my leave. Know'st thou whom thou slightest? I am a man of whom the roarers * stand in awe and must not be put off.

BESS: I never yet heard man so praise himself but proved in the end a coward.

PURSER (*seizing her again roughly*): Coward, Bess! You will offend me, raise in me that fury your beauty cannot calm. Your language is too harsh. I tell thee, that day scarce passed me these seven years, I have not cracked a weapon in some fray; and will you move my spleen?

ALL: What, threat a woman? Fie! fie! (*They pull* PURSER *away.*)

BESS: Can we not live in compass of the law, but must be swaggered out on't?

* Evidently alluding to Town criers.

Purser: Go to, wench, I wish thee well. There's good for thee stored in my breast, but when I come in place I must have no man to offend mine eye. My love can brook no rivals. For *this* time I am content your captains shall have peace, but must not be used to it.

Bess: Sir, if you come here like other free * and civil gentlemen, you're welcome, otherwise the doors are barred you.

Purser: I have fortunes laid up. What I have, command it as thine own. Consider on't, my good girl — farewell.

(Exit, followed by all.)

Bess: My mind suggests me this prating fellow is some notorious coward.

(Uproar outside.) Enter 1st Drawer.

1st Drawer: Bess, you must needs come; the gentlemen fling pots, pottle, drawers and all, down stairs. The whole house is in an uproar.

(Exit Bess.)

Enter Rainsforth, Goodwin, *and* Foster.

Rainsforth: Boy, my cloak.

Goodwin: Our cloaks, sirrah.

Foster: Why, Drawer!

1st Drawer: Here, sir.

Rainsforth: Some canary, sack and tobacco.

1st Drawer: You shall, sir. Wilt please you stay to supper?

Rainsforth: Yes, marry, will we, sir. Let's have the best cheer the kitchen yields. The pipe, sirrah.

Drawer: Here, sir.

(Exit.)

Rainsforth: Will Frank be here at supper?

Goodwin: So, sir, he promised and presumes he will not fail his hour.

Rainsforth: Some sack, boy. I am all lead within. There's no mirth in me, nor was I wont to be so lumpish sad. *(To the boy who has brought the wine)* Reach me the glass. What's this?

2nd Drawer: Good sherry sack, sir.

* Independent.

RAINSFORTH: I meant canary, sir. What, hast no brains? (*Throws wine on floor.*)

2ND DRAWER: To the devil with your brains! Are your fingers so light?

RAINSFORTH: What d'ye say, sir?

2ND DRAWER: You shall have canary presently. (*Exit.*)

GOODWIN: When was he wont to be in this sad strain? Excepting some few sudden melancholies, there lives not one more free and sociable.

FOSTER: I am too well acquainted with his humor to stir his blood in the least distemperature. (*To* RAINSFORTH) Cozen, I'll sit with you here.

RAINSFORTH: Do come to me. (*To* DRAWER *who enters*) Have you hit upon the right canary now or could your hogshead find a Spanish Butt? (*To his friends*) A health!

GOODWIN: Were it my height, I'll pledge it. (*Drinks.*)

FOSTER: How do you now, man?

RAINSFORTH: Well, well, exceedingly well. My melancholy sadness steals away, and by degrees shrinks from my troubled heart. Come, let's be merry. More tobacco, boy, and bring in supper.

Enter FRANK FORREST.

FOSTER: Welcome, Frank, welcome. Wilt thou sit here, old lad?

GOODWIN: Or here?

FRANK: Wherefore hath nature lent me two hands but to use them both at once? My cloak. I am for you here and here. (*Removes cloak and gives it to boy — then sits by* GOODWIN.)

FOSTER (*to* DRAWER): Bid them make haste with supper. (*To* GOODWIN *and* FRANK) Some discourse to pass away the time.

RAINSFORTH: Now, Frank, how stole you from your father's arms? You have been schooled, no doubt. Fie, fie upon 't, ere I would live in such base servitude to an old graybeard, 'sfoot, I'd hang myself. A man cannot be merry and drink drunk, but he must be controlled by gravity.

FRANK: O, pardon him, you know he is my father and what he doth is but paternal love. Though I be wild, I am not so past reason his person to despise, though I his counsel cannot severely follow.

RAINSFORTH: 'S foot, he's a fool.

FRANK: A fool! You're a —

FOSTER: Nay, gentlemen!

FRANK: I restrain my tongue hoping you speak out of some spleenful rashness, and no deliberate malice. And 't may be you are sorry that a word so unreverent, to wrong so good an aged gentleman, should pass you unawares.

RAINSFORTH: Sorry, sir boy! You will not take exceptions?

FRANK: Not against you with willingness, whom I have loved so long. Yet you might think me a most ungracious son to give smooth countenance unto my father's wrong. Come, I dare swear it was not in malice and I take it so. Let's frame some other talk. Here, gentlemen!

RAINSFORTH: But hear me, boy. It seems, sir, you *are* angry.

FRANK: Not yet.

RAINSFORTH: Then what would anger thee?

FRANK: Nothing from you.

RAINSFORTH: Of all things under heaven, what would'st thou loathest have me do?

FRANK: I would not have you wrong my father and I hope you will not.

RAINSFORTH: Thy father's an old dotard.

FRANK (*starting to his feet*): I could not brook this at a monarch's hands, much less at thine.

RAINSFORTH (*mockingly*): Ay, boy, then take you that. (*Flings wine in his face;* FRANK *draws sword,* RAINSFORTH *does the same quickly.*)

FRANK: I was not born to brook this. Oh! I'm slain. (*Falls dead.*)

GOODWIN: Sweet coz, what have you done? Shift for your self.

FOSTER: Away. (*They hurry* RAINSFORTH *out. As they do so, the* DRAWERS *enter carrying supper, see* FRANK'S *body, and call out.*)

1ST DRAWER: Oh! stay the gentlemen; they have killed a man.

Enter BESS *who runs to* FRANK *and kneels beside him. The* DRAWERS *come to her.*

1ST DRAWER: O, sweet Mr. Francis!

2D DRAWER: They have drawn the blood of this gentleman that I have drawn many a quart of wine to.

BESS: What! Are you men or milksops? Stand you still, senseless as stones, and see a man expire his last? One call my master, another fetch a constable!

1ST DRAWER: Hark, I hear his father's voice below; ten to one he is come to fetch him home to supper and now he may carry him home to his grave.— See, here he comes.

BESS and the others draw aside as MR. FORREST *and* SUSAN *and the* HOST *enter.*

HOST: You must take comfort, sir.

OLD FORREST: Would Heaven I could.

SUSAN: Oh! my brother. (*Kneels by* FRANK, *weeping and wringing her hands.*)

OLD FORREST: Is he dead, is he dead, girl?

SUSAN: Ay, dead, sir. Frank is dead.

OLD FORREST: Alas, alas, my boy! (*Falls into chair by table.*) I have not the heart to look upon his wide and gaping wounds. (*Turning to* HOST.) Pray tell me, sir, doth this appear to you fearful and pitiful, to you who are a stranger to my dead boy?

HOST: How can it be otherwise?

OLD FORREST: If to a stranger his wounds appear so lamentable, how will they seem to me that am his father? (*Goes toward body.*) Ah me, is this my son that doth so senseless lie? My soul shall fly with his into the land of rest. Behold, I crave, being killed with grief, we both have one grave. (*Falls senseless across body of his son.*)

SUSAN: Alas, my father is dead, too, gentle sir. Help to restore his spirit, over travailed with age and sorrow.

HOST (*trying to rouse* MR. FORREST): Mr. Forrest! sir!

SUSAN: Father!

OLD FORREST (*looking at her smiling and in a dazed manner*): What says my girl? Good morrow, what's o'clock that you are up so early? Call up Frank; tell him he lies too long abed this morning. Will he not up? Rise, rise, thou sluggish boy!

SUSAN: Alas, father, he cannot.

OLD FORREST: Cannot, why?

SUSAN: Do you not feel his pulse no motion keep?

OLD FORREST (*bursting into tears*): Ah, me! my murdered son!

(*Enter* YOUNG FORREST *who rushes to* SUSAN *and his father.*)

YOUNG FORREST: Sister!

SUSAN: Brother!

YOUNG FORREST: Father, how cheer you, sir? Why, you were wont to store for others' comfort, that by sorrow were any way distressed. Have you all wasted, and spared none for yourself?

OLD FORREST: Oh, son! son! See, alas, where thy brother lies. He dined with me to-day, was merry, merry, he that lies there. See thy murdered brother. Dost thou not weep for him?

YOUNG FORREST: When you have taken some comfort, I'll begin to mourn his death and scourge the murderers' sin. Dear father, be advised, take hence the body and let it have solemn funeral.

OLD FORREST: But the murderer? Shall not he attend the sentence of the law with all severity?

YOUNG FORREST: Have you but patience. Should we urge the law, he hath such honourable friends to guard him, we should but bark against the moon. Let the law sleep. The time, ere it be long, may offer itself to a more just revenge. We are poor and the world frowns on all our fortune. With patience then bear this amongst the rest. Heaven, when it please, may turn the wheel of fortune round, when we that are dejected may again be raised to our former height.

OLD FORREST: Oh! when saw father such a tragic sight and did outlive it?

YOUNG FORREST (*leading his father away*): Nay, do not look that way. (*To* DRAWERS) Bear hence the body. (*They stand beside it, ready to bear it off.*) Come, father, and, dear sister, join with me. He owed a death and he hath paid the debt. (*Men bear away body as curtain falls.*)

ACT II.

SCENE I.—*Garden in front of* MR. HARDING'S *house. House L. and near it thatched cabin or henhouse.*

Enter MR. HARDING, *his sons* WILLIAM *and* JOHN, *and his wife* ANN, *newly arrived from the wedding, followed by wedding procession.*

MR. HARDING: So! things are as they should be, sweet Nan. We have attained the height of solace and true joy. What I lack in youth I will make good in wealth.

ANN: Sir, you well know I was not easily won. Advisedly, not rashly, did I venture on your love. My young unsettled thoughts from their long travels have late attained unto their journey's end and they are now at rest.

MR. HARDING: Here they have found a harbour to retire to.

WILLIAM: 'Twould become you to use my father here respectfully.* You see how he receives you, almost dowerless.

JOHN: True, where he out of his own abilities might have commanded widows of rich estate,† ay and perhaps as beautiful.

ANN: Upbraid me not. I do confess he might; nor was this match my seeking. If it hath pleased your father, for some virtues known in me to grace me with his free election, methinks it worse becomes you, being sons, to blame a father's pleasure. Howsoever, better myself I cannot; if he thought me worthy, I see small reason you should wrong me to him that best knew my state.

MR. HARDING: Nan, I am pleased they shall be satisfied; and, boys, I tell you, though you be my sons, you much forget your duty to a mother whom I hold worthy to be called my wife. No more of this, I charge you.

WILL: Sir, we have done.

MR. HARDING: No child to *her* can be to *me* no son.

JOHN: I am satisfied; here my spleen dies as suddenly fallen as it did quickly rise.

---

* Original "respectively."   † Original "farre."

MR. HARDING: This is the end I aimed at; were my eldest present among us, I had my height of wishes.

Enter CLOWN.

CLOWN: I have been there, sir.

MR. HARDING: And foundest thou my son Philip?

CLOWN: When you had given him me in charge, I had of him great care, and I have took him napping. I found your son Philip billing like a cock sparrow. I know not whether it be St. Valentine's day or no, but I am sure they are coupled.

MR. HARDING: How coupled dost thou mean?

CLOWN: I see them one and one, and that you know makes two, and two makes a couple. I think 'tis like to be a match.

MR. HARDING: I vow if e'er he match into that family, the kindred being all beggared, that union shall make a firm divorce 'twixt him and me.

WILL: 'Tis true, upon my life.

MR. HARDING: Say what thou wilt, I'll not believe it, boy.

WILL: Do you believe me to be your son William?

MR. HARDING: Well.

WILLIAM: Do you believe I stand here?

MR. HARDING: On.

WILL: That this gentlewoman is your wife?

MR. HARDING: So.

WILL: That Jack Harding here is my brother?

MR. HARDING: Good.

WILL: That I speak to you, that you list to me? Do you believe anything that is to be believed?

MR. HARDING: What of all this?

WILL: Then believe my brother Philip has married mistress Susan. I saw them in the church together. I heard them pronounce the words. Whether it be better or worse for them I know not, but they are in for better or for worse; that I am sure.

MR. HARDING: As sure as thou art certain this is true, so sure I'll disinherit the proud boy and all the store* that I enjoy divide 'tween you my sons.

JOHN: Not all, father. Alas, allow him some small legacy to live on.

* Original "magazin."

WILL: If it be but a cast-off farm, or some poor cottage, rather than nothing. It may be he'll content himself with a little; you know somewhat hath some savour.*

MR. HARDING: He that hath set me and my love at nothing, I'll leave him worth as little.

ANN: Chide him you may, but yet not cast him off. Parents, as I have read, their rage should hide where children fall through weakness, not through pride.

MR. HARDING: They are none such to me. My vow is passed. My life may fade but still my will shall last.

CLOWN: Here they are, sir, *coram nobis;* you will find it a plain case. I have spoke but what I have seen and now let every one answer for himself.

Enter PHILIP *and* SUSAN.

MR. HARDING: What mean these hands?

PHILIP: Nothing, sir, save a mere interchange of hearts and souls, made doubly fast by vows.

MR. HARDING: 'Twixt her and thee?

PHILIP: So, and no other.

MR. HARDING: Yet, thou hast time. Cast her off or henceforth I disclaim thee for my son.

PHILIP: Yet I shall ever hold you for my father.

MR. HARDING: Then show in this thy duty. Forsake her and be restored unto thy family.

PHILIP: Sir, that Power above, that heard the contract pass, both heard, approved and still records the same. Oh, sir, I am of age;† oft have you wished to see me well bestowed. It was your prayer that Heaven should send me a good wife and lo! in her it has shown its bounty.

MR. HARDING: Thou, thy baseness. Take one of my choosing.

PHILIP: Do men use others' hearts and eyes to choose their wives?

MR. HARDING: She's poor.

PHILIP: Yet hath many virtues.

MR. HARDING: Virtues! A sweet dower! Possessed of vir-

* Old proverb, " Somewhat has some savour, but nothing has no flavour."

† Original, " years."

tue, then, thou needst naught else. Go to Cheapside with virtue in your purse and see what meat with virtue you can buy. Will virtue make the pot boil? Tell me will your landlord at quarter-day take virtue for his rent? Come, come, son, I'll find thee a rich match; turn her off.

WILL: 'Faith, do, brother; the only way to thrive is to be ruled by my father.

JACK: Do you think I would marry without my father's consent?

PHILIP: I hope you may not, but withal advise you have a conscience how you break a vow. And sir, for you, with pardon, I could trace you in that path in which I stand condemned. This gentlewoman, whom in no kind I envy, I presume you married not for riches, for if so where is the wealthy dower she brought along? In viewing me, bear but yourself in mind, and prove to her, as I to this, (*kisses* ANN's *hand*) like kind.

ANN: The gentleman speaks well; pray, let me mediate between you a reconcilement. Sir, he is your son and of your blood the first. Though you have power to take away his means, deprive him not your blessing and your love, which, methinks, in a father should seem strange. His state you may, his blood you cannot, change.

MR. HARDING: Have I been thus long a father, and a master to direct, to be at these years pupill'd by a girl — a beggar, — one that all the wealth she has bears on her back? She that ought to arm me with just rage preaches to me patience. Shall I suffer this? I'll endure no more. By all that I enjoy —

PHILIP: Swear not, spare that oath. I'll credit you, though you speak but mildly.

MR. HARDING: So may I thrive, if, for this marriage made in despite of me, I make thee partner of any substance that's accounted mine.

PHILIP: Not made in spite of you; unsay that language, sir. I matched with her in sincere love but in no spleen to you. Though you have sworn to give my fortune from me, you have not sworn to spoil * me of your love. That let me have; let others take the land.

* Original "reave."

MR. HARDING: My love goes with my land and in this marriage thou hast lost both.

ANN: Oh, bear a soft and more relenting soul; look upon the virtues of your son and this gentlewoman's birth.

MR. HARDING: Wife, wife, if he have married her for birth, then let her birth maintain him.

ANN: My kind sons, speak to your father.

WILL: Alas, mother, you hear my father hath sworn, and would you who love him make him break his oath?

JOHN: Pawn * his soul. That were a wife's part, indeed.

WILL: As I live I would not wish him, now he has sworn, to alter his mind in the least circumstance.

PHILIP: I am a kinder son than you be brothers. Have you renounced me for your son?

MR. HARDING: I have.

PHILIP: You have not yet renounced me for your servant. That title let me bear. Since poverty enforces me to serve, let it be you.

WILL: Grant him that, good father. When you lack employment for him I may sometimes have occasion to use him myself.

JOHN: You need a serving man, and since you must hire one, so good him as another.

PHILIP: He needs a maid too — let him hire this woman. Give us as you would do to strangers, we are satisfied.

WILL: The motion's not amiss. Can you milk, sweetheart?

SUSAN: I can.

WILL: And sweep a house?

SUSAN: What I have done, my soft hand best can show. What I know not I'll be glad to learn.

MR. HARDING (*to* PHILIP): Sirrah, can you hold a plough and thrash, sow, reap, load a cart and drive a team?

PHILIP: These or what else I'll practise.

MR. HARDING: Come then, off with these gay clothes not fit for hinds. Help, boys, to suit them as their fortunes are. Go, search in the clown's wardrobe.

WILL: Fear not, we'll fit them as well as if we'd ta'en measure of them —

(*Exeunt both.*)

* Original " Ingage."

ANN: To see such misery with such patience borne makes me pity where these others scorn. (*Crosses quickly to* SUSAN *and unobserved kisses her. Re-enter* JOHN *and* WILLIAM *with clothes which they display.*)

JOHN: Here, sir, is that will serve the turn. If you employ him in the cornfields, I'll warrant him fright the birds.

WILL: And here's that will change the copy of her case though not her countenance.

MR. HARDING (*throwing clothes towards* PHILIP *and* SUSAN): Too good for drudges. Live now by your sweat, and by your labor make account to eat.

(*Exeunt all into house except* CLOWN, PHILIP, *and* SUSAN.)

CLOWN: Oh, most tyrannical old master. Well, since it is no more young master but fellow servant, no more Master Philip but "Phil," here's my hand. I'll do two men's labour in one to save you labour, and to spare your shoulders I'll help at many a dead lift. Come, I'll teach you the name of all our stock and acquaint you with all the God-a-mercy fraternity. To see so brave a gentleman turn clown!

(*Exit.*)

PHILIP (*taking* SUSAN *in his arms*): Here's but a sorry wedding day, sweetheart. Alas for thee that thou must toil and drudge, and having been a mistress all thy life, must now become a servant.

SUSAN: My sweet Philip, that thou shouldst suffer these extremes for me, only for me!

PHILIP: Let that betwixt my soul and thine be witness of my true love.

CURTAIN.

ACT II.

SCENE 2.— *A street same as first scene.*

(*Enter R. and L.,* RAINSFORTH *and* YOUNG FORREST.)

FORREST: Pray let me speak with you.

RAINSFORTH: With me, sir?

FORREST: Do you not know me?

RAINSFORTH: Keep off upon the peril of thy life lest this arm prove fatal to thee, and take thy life, as it hath done thy brother's.

FORREST: Thou knowest me truly by that token. Put up, put up, so great a quarrel as a brother's life must not be made a street brawl. Sheathe thy sword.

RAINSFORTH: Swear thou wilt act no sudden violence or this sharp sword shall still be interposed 'twixt me and thy known hatred.

FORREST: Sheathe thy sword. By my religion, I will not be guilty of any base revenge. Let not thy guilty soul be jealous of my fury. My hand is curbed and governed by an honest heart, not by just anger.

RAINSFORTH (*sheathes sword*): Proceed.

FORREST: Sir, you did kill my brother. Had it been in fair and even encounter, his death I had not questioned.

RAINSFORTH: Is this all?

FORREST: He's gone, the law is past, your life is clear; for none of all our kindred laid against you evidence to hang you. You are a gentleman and pity 'twere a man of your descent should die a felon's death. Thus far we have demeaned fairly, like ourselves; but think you a brother's death can be so soon forgot, our gentry baffled and our name disgraced? I am a gentleman, well known, and should I swallow this, the scandal would outlive me. Briefly then I'd fight with you. Answer directly, whether you dare to meet me on even terms.

RAINSFORTH: Say I refuse?

FORREST: Then *I* say thou art a villain and I challenge thee where'er I meet thee next, in field or town, thy father's manor or thy tenants' grange; saving the church there is no privilege in all this land for thy despis'd life. No guard of friends, no jealous fear, which in a murderer's eye keeps hourly watch, shall save thee. I'll *kill* thee, be it in thy bed or abroad; in thy wife's arms or at meat, as thou didst my brother. Answer me.

RAINSFORTH: I'll meet with thee. The hour?

FORREST: By six to-morrow morning. 'Tis your privilege to appoint the place and weapon.

RAINSFORTH: Hownslow the place, my choice of weapon this.

FORREST: I can except at neither. Farewell.

(Exit.)

RAINSFORTH: 'Tis thou meetest thy last farewell on earth. The appointed hour is to-morrow. Let the same fate obscure his desperate head that fell upon his brother's.

Enter GOODWIN and FOSTER.

GOODWIN: Now, Cozen Rainsforth.

RAINSFORTH (*still looking in the direction that* FORREST *took*): I'll so swinge my yonker.*

FOSTER: Why, who hath raised this storm, sir?

RAINSFORTH: Young Forrest, parted but even now, called me to question 'bout his brother's death and since hath challenged me.

GOODWIN: Challenged?

RAINSFORTH (*laughing*): Challenged *me*.

FOSTER: Why, he's too weak for you.

RAINSFORTH: My purpose is to teach the stripling sense. And you be honest gentlemen stand but aloof to-morrow and observe how I will swinge my youth about the field.

GOODWIN: I'll be there.

FOSTER: And so will I. (*Exeunt*).

RAINSFORTH: He seeks his fate, and murderers, once being in, wade further till they drown. Sin pulls on sin.

CURTAIN.

ACT III.

SCENE I.— Garden. Same as Act II.

Enter WILLIAM and PHILIP.

WILL: Now wilt truss me that point, Phil? I could find it in my heart to beg thee of my father to wait on me, but that I am afraid he cannot spare thee from the plough. Besides, I heard him say but the last day, thou wast more fit to make a hind than a serving man.

* Whip my youngster.

PHILIP : Sir, you were once my brother.

WILL : True, but that was when you were son to my father; but now it seems we have got the start of you for being but a servant you are taken a button-hole lower.

PHILIP : When will this tedious night give place to-day?

WILL : I hope I may command.

PHILIP : I must obey. (*Laces doublet.*)

Enter JOHN *and* SUSAN.

JOHN : My string, Sue. Are these shoes well cleaned?* Down on your marrow bones, good Sue. I hope you're not so straight-laced you cannot stoop. You acknowledge me one of your young masters; if not, I know the way to my father.

SUSAN : Yes, sir, and can tell tales. I know you can and I have felt the smart on't.

JOHN : Whip me if you shall not, if you begin once to grow stubborn.

(SUSAN *kneels to tie his shoe as* ANN *enters.*)

ANN : How now, maid, is this work fitting you? And you, sir, (*to* PHILIP) you are looked for in the stable.

PHILIP : I am for any service.

SUSAN : And I, too.

ANN : We shall find other things for you to do.

(*Exeunt.*)

WILL : If you cannot, here be they that can.

JOHN : And if I do not find work for her, I'll take tobacco in every room and twice a day will make her clean the house.

(*Exeunt.*)

ANN : To see them thus afflicted grates my very heartstrings every hour. Though before their father's pitiless † eye, and their remorseless brothers', I seem stern, yet privately they taste my best bounty; and other of my servants are hired by me to perform ‡ their chiefest drudgery. (*Sits at her embroidery frame and begins to work.*)

(*Enter* YOUNG FORREST *running with his sword drawn.*)

* Original " mundified."   † Original " rathless."
‡ Original " overcome."

YOUNG FORREST: I am pursued and there is no place of refuge; but here's a woman. If she harbour soft effeminate pity, she may redeem me from a shameful death. Sweet lady —

ANN: A man thus armed to leap my garden wall! Help! help!

FORREST: As you are fair and should be pitiful — a woman, therefore to be moved — a Christian and therefore one that should be charitable — pity a poor distressed gentleman who gives his desperate fortune, life and freedom into your hands.

ANN: What are you, sir, that with your weapon drawn, affright me thus?

FORREST: If you protect my life, fair lady, I am a free gentleman, but, if you betray me, then a poor man doomed unto a shameful death.

ANN: What's your offence, that such suspicious fear and timorous doubts wait on your guilty steps?

FORREST: I have killed a man (ANN *starts back in horror*) but fairly, as I am a gentleman, in even trial of both our desperate fortunes.

ANN: Fairly?

FORREST: And though I say it, valiantly.

ANN: And hand to hand?

FORREST: In single opposition.

ANN: In a good quarrel?

FORREST: Else let the hope I have in you of safety, turn to my confusion. (*Distant voices outside.*) Gentle lady, I cannot now stand to expostulate, for hark, the breath of my pursuers blows a fearful air upon my flying steel and I am almost in their fatal grasp. Will you save me?

ANN: I will,— climb into that hovel.

FORREST: Anywhere.

ANN: Nay, quickly then.

FORREST: Your hand, fair lady.

ANN: Away! leave me to answer for you. (*Sits again at work.*)

Enter MR. HARDING, GOODWIN, FOSTER *and officers.*

MR. HARDING: Over my garden wall! is't possible?

GOODWIN: I saw him leap it lightly.

Mr. Harding: That shall we quickly know. See, here's my wife, she can best inform us.

Foster: Saw you not, Mistress Harding, a young man mount o'er this garden wall with his sword drawn?

Ann: My eyes were steadfast on my work in hand; trust me, I saw none.

Mr. Harding: Perhaps he altered his course and took to the neighbouring village when he saw my wife.

Ann: 'Tis very like so, for I heard a bustling about that hedge, besides a sudden noise of some that swiftly ran towards yon fields. Make haste, 'twas now, he cannot be far off.

Mr. Harding: Gentlemen, take my word; I am high constable and will be no shelter for any man that shall offend the law. If you surprise him I will send him bound to the nearest justice. Follow you your search.

Goodwin: Farewell, good Mr. Harding.

Foster (to Harding): Your word's sufficient without further warrant. (To officers) Continue our pursuit. All ways are laid and ere he reach the city hall he shall be staid.

(Exeunt.)

Mr. Harding: Adieu, good friends.

Ann: Pray, what's the business, sir?

Mr. Harding: Two gentlemen went into the fields to fight and one hath slain the other.

Ann: On what quarrel?

Mr. Harding: Only this much I learnt. The man that's dead was great in fault, and he that now survives, bore himself fairly. But his fortune being to kill a man allied to noblemen and greatly friended, is much to be pitied; but the law must have its course. Come, the morning's bleak and sharp the air,—in to the fire, my girl, there is wholesome heat. I'll in and see my servants set at meat.

Ann: Sir, I'll but finish this flower and follow you. (Exit Mr. Harding.) If this be true I thank my fate and bless this happy hour to save a life within law's gripping power. Great were my guilt to shield him from the law if this should prove some bloody murderer, but if a gentleman by fortune crossed 'tis pity one so valiant and so young, should be given up into his enemies' hands. Their greatness may perhaps weigh down his cause and balance him to death, who thus escaping, may, when he hath by means obtained his peace, redeem his desperate fortunes, and make good the forfeit made unto the offended law. Prove as Heaven shall direct, I'll do my best, 'tis charity to succour the distressed.

FORREST (*looking out*): Young Mistress, are they gone? May I depart?

ANN: No safety lies abroad; then pray forbear to speak of 'scaping hence.

FORREST: Oh! but I fear.

ANN: My life for yours.

FORREST: However poor I fare, may you for this charitable care taste happy fruit.

ANN (*earnestly*): You did not kill him foully?

FORREST: No! I protest.

ANN: Nor willingly?

FORREST: I willingly fought with him, but unwillingly did I become his deathsman.

ANN: Could you now wish him alive again?

FORREST: With his hands free — and yet he slew my brother.

ANN: Heaven hath sent this gentleman to me for succour, therefore till the violence of all his search be passed I'll shield him here. I'll bring you meat and wine to comfort you till by some means I may convey you hence.

FORREST: The life you save, if I o'ercome this plunge, shall be forever yours. All my endeavours to your devoted service I will store and carefully hoard up. (*Kisses her hand fervently.*)

ANN (*agitatedly*): Sir, no more.

(*Exeunt.*)

Enter CLOWN *and* PHILIP.

CLOWN: Come, good fellow Phil. What, nothing but mourning and moping? Thy melancholy makes all our jades crest-fallen, and my mistress Susan is in the same pitiful pickle.

PHILIP: Oh, if this hand could execute for her all that my cruel father doth impose, my toil would seem a pleasure, labour ease.

CLOWN: Ease, what's that? There's little to be found in our house. Now we have loosed the plough in the fields they'll find work enough about home to keep us from the scurvy. Your hat, Phil; see, here comes our mistress.

Enter ANN *with bread and a bottle.*

ANN : How now, fellows, whither so fast this way ? (*Stands in front of hovel.*)

CLOWN : Nay, we do not go too fast for falling ; our business at present is about a little household service.

ANN : What business have you this way ?

PHILIP : By my master's order, I must not say my father's, he hath commanded us first to make clean this hen roost and after to remove the hay out of that loft.

ANN (*aside*): Ah, me, I fear the gentleman's betrayed. What shift shall I devise ?

CLOWN : By your leave, mistress, pray let's come by you.

ANN : Well, double diligence has your labour saved. 'Tis done already ; go and take your pleasure. Son Philip, when I heard my husband speak of such base employment, I straight hired a labourer to prevent it, and 'tis done.

PHILIP : You are kinder, mother, than my father is cruel, and save me many a toil.

ANN : Will you both be gone?

CLOWN : Yes, sweet mistress, if you would but give a wink, a word, to the dairy maid for a mess of cream 'twixt my fellow Phil and I. It's good to be doing something, for you know my master does not like we should be idle.

ANN : Well, sir, perhaps I shall remember you.

CLOWN : Come, Phil, let's be gone.

(*Exeunt.*)

ANN : Shall I compare his misery with this gentleman's, which might I reckon greater ? Ah, me, we all must yield to fate. He casts us down who best can raise our state. (*Enter* SUSAN *with something in her apron.*) Again prevented. What business have you here ?

SUSAN : Forsooth, my master bade me serve the poultry.

ANN : You shall not. For this time I'll do it for you.

SUSAN : Mother and mistress, 'tis kind in you to proffer, but should I suffer it you might justly hold me in small manners.

ANN : I say it shall be so.

SUSAN : Shall I stand idly and see the work done by your hand !

ANN : I say I will.

SUSAN: My words dare not say nay, but my more froward action brooks no stay. (*She pushes past* ANN *and enters hovel.*)

ANN: Doubtless he's betrayed.

SUSAN (*running out frightened*): Ah me, here's one that comes to steal your hens. Shall I cry thief?

ANN: For Heaven's sake, no.

Enter YOUNG FORREST.

FORREST: Once more I lie ordained for pity or prepared to die. (*Looking around*) What! none but women, and betray me?

ANN: Think not that I'll betray you nor shall she, if she respect my love or her own life.

SUSAN: Betray my brother! (*Rushes to him.*)

FORREST: Oh, fortune beyond hope! Amazed I stand to see my life laid in my sister's hand.

ANN: Her brother? Strange greeting and 'twixt two hapless creatures happy meeting.

FORREST: What change hath brought you to this downcast state?

SUSAN: Nay, what mishap hath ruined you?

ANN: You both forget your dangers. Leave off and study for the safety of this distressed gentleman, your brother, now in the ruthless mercy of the law.

FORREST: Sister, you have heard my fortunes?

SUSAN: With sad cheer, little surmising you had lain so near. Dear mother, let's crave your farther assistance in furthering his escape.

ANN: I am all yours.

FORREST: My safety lies in sudden expedition.

ANN: I have a brother at Gravesend, an owner and a merchant; could we but convey thee safe to him, he soon would ship you over into France.

FORREST: All ways are loud with hue and cry; alas, how shall I reach thither without discovery?

SUSAN: There stands an empty trunk within which should be sent by water to Gravesend to your brother; what if we should lock him fast in that?

ANN: I like it well, but whom shall we employ to bear it safe?

SUSAN: Give it my husband and your man in charge; they two will see it carefully delivered.

ANN: By them I'll write unto him earnestly in your behalf, and doubt not of your voyage.

FORREST: Your trunk then, quickly if you love me.

ANN: I'll go to write.

SUSAN: I'll send those that shall bear it.

FORREST: The plot is likely but Heaven knows I fear it.

Exit ANN *into house,* SUSAN *and* FORREST *into hovel.*

Enter old MR. FORREST *bent and half weeping.*

OLD FORREST: Alas, alas, my children, those that seven summers since saw thy estate and looked upon thee now, would at least pity if not help thy wants. How happy was thy mother who slept her last sleep long before these sorrows took their birth. (*Enter* MR. HARDING.) You are well found, sir.

MR. HARDING: I — what art thou, fellow?

OLD FORREST: You knew me in my pride and flourishing state; have you forgot me now? As I remember, we two were bred together as school fellows: boarded together in one master's house, both of one form and like degree in school.

MR. HARDING: Oh, thy name's Forrest.

OLD FORREST: In those days, your father, Mr. Harding, was a good honest farmer, tenant too unto my father, and you called me then your landlord and young master. Then was then, but now, the course of fortune's wheel is turned. You climbed, we fell, and that inconstant fate that hurled us down hath lift you to where we sate.

MR. HARDING: Well, we are lord of all those manors now, you then possessed. Have we not bought them dearly? Are they not ours?

OLD FORREST: I no way can deny it; I come rather as a poor suitor to you, to entreat you for Heaven's sake and Charity's to pity my daughter. She is yours as well as mine.

MR. HARDING: All my part I disclaim both in my son and her. They crossed my pleasure and they shall taste the smart.

OLD FORREST: Sir, if your heart be not of adamant, or some hard metal that's impenetrable, pity your blood and mine.

MR. HARDING (*impatiently*): Thou grow'st too tedious; prithee, friend, begone.

OLD FORREST: I hope you do not scorn me.

MR. HARDING: The truth is, I fain would have thee leave me.

OLD FORREST: 'Tis no disparagement unto your birth that you converse with me. If I mistake not, sure, I am as well born.

MR. HARDING: And yet, sure, sure, 'tis ten to one I shall be better buried.

OLD FORREST: I am as honest.

MR. HARDING: Nay, there you are aground. I am honester by twenty thousand pound.

OLD FORREST: Are all such honest then, that riches have?

MR. HARDING: Yes, rich and good, a poor man and a knave. Away about thy business and loiter not about my gates else I compel thee hence.

OLD FORREST: Gentry and baseness in all ages jar, and poverty and wealth are still at war.

(*As curtain goes down* OLD FORREST *walks out of gate and* MR. HARDING *angrily enters house.*)

CURTAIN.

ACT IV.

SCENE I.—*Interior front drop.*

Enter MERCHANT *and* YOUNG FORREST.

MERCHANT: My sister writes how your occasions stand and how you are to use my secrecy in a strange business that concerns your life. She hath left nothing unremembered here or slightly urged to make me careful of your safety. Gentle sir, though I am a stranger to you, yet for her sake whose love I tender dearly I am all yours. My house to entertain you, my purse to furnish you, my ship, if you'll to sea, is at your service.

Make choice in which of these, in all or any, you will employ
my faithful industry.

FORREST: Sir, your unexpected courtesies to a poor stranger
challenges the name of brother to the kindest gentlewoman
that ever breathed this air. You bade me make choice of all
your favors. My poverty and my necessity do make me think
the meanest of any means that can unplunge me from this gulf
of trouble to be much better than I deserve, much greater than
I dare desire.

MERCHANT: You wrong your worth; you have desert sufficient; that she writes in your behalf, and I commend her for it.
Methinks I see such honest parts in you that, upon weaker
urgence than these lines, I would build much affection on these
gifts. Indeed I flatter not; none flatter those they do not
mean to gain by.

FORREST: If ever my weak ability grow strong again, may I
never be guilty of the base sin of ingratitude towards you and
your fair sister.

MERCHANT: Will you make use of me? Pray let me know
what I may do.

FORREST: Then sir, will you provide me a safe waftage over
to France, to Flanders, to Spain or any foreign coast? I dare
not trust my native country with my forfeit life.

MERCHANT: You're modest in your suit. This night I'll get
your waftage o'er to France. Of such sea apparel as I use myself you shall accept a part. Here's ten pounds in gold, and
wheresoever you shall live hereafter, pray let me once a year
receive from you some brief or note. I'll not return your love
idle or empty handed.

FORREST: My life is yours, and lesser satisfaction than my
life is much too little.

MERCHANT (laughing): Much too much. No more I do entreat you. I am now upon a voyage to the straits myself but
'twill be two days hence.

FORREST: Heaven be your guide, and as I find you, so find
you friends in need.

MERCHANT: Come, we'll provide for your safe waftage and
your secret flight.

(Exeunt.)

ACT IV.

SCENE 2.— *Landscape — Drop scene.*

Enter CLOWN, FOSTER, *and* GOODWIN.

FOSTER: Speak with us? Why, what's the business?

CLOWN: Nay, that's more than I can tell* you upon the sudden. It may be there's some great fortune fallen to him of late, and he would impart the benefit to you.

GOODWIN: Nay then, let's go. Where shall we find him?

CLOWN: A word to the wise. It may be that he's in some monstrous extreme necessity and would gladly borrow some money of you.

GOODWIN (*to* FOSTER): Ay, said'st thou so? (*To* CLOWN) Now I remember me I needs must home, I have some business. I'll see him some other time.

CLOWN: Nay, but one word more.

FOSTER: We cannot stay now.

CLOWN: Nay, then, I see you are apt to take a man at the worst; still if you knew what little need he had to borrow. "Borrow," quoth he, "a good jest." You know he and I, my fellow Phil and I, 'mongst other work that my master put us to, used to dig and delve;—now if we have found a pot of money and would trust you with the laying out of it, how then?

FOSTER: How?

CLOWN: Marry, even so. You know his father is such a dogged old curmudgeon, he dares not for his ears acquaint him with it.

GOODWIN: Prithee, go on.

CLOWN: 'Twere kindness in him to choose you, out of all the friends he hath in the world, to impart this benefit to, were it not?

FOSTER: Troth, he was always a kind honest youth, and I would pleasure him.

GOODWIN: Where might we speak with him?

CLOWN: Hard by; but stay, gentlemen, suppose there is no

* Original "resolve."

such matter as finding of money, but what we missed in digging to supply his present necessities he hopes to find in you. I promise you I partly doubt such a matter.

GOODWIN: H'm! I forgot myself; I needs must home.

FOSTER: And I.

Enter PHILIP *meeting them.*

PHILIP: Gentlemen, whither so fast? I sent to speak with you.

CLOWN: I can assure you, sir, they are better to speak withal than to borrow money of. My friends, one word with you. By your leave, master. Gentlemen, I love you well and that you may know I love you I would make bold to reveal a secret to you. My young master here, though you see him in these homely accoutrements might go brave, and shine in pearl and gold. He hath now in his possession, at least in his reach (*touching the two men on the shoulders*) a thousand pounds.

FOSTER: A thousand pounds!

CLOWN: Nay, old lads, he hath learnt his 1-2-3-4-5- and never cost him ten shillings.

GOODWIN: Five thousand pounds!

CLOWN: Now lift up your large ears and listen. To whom should he reveal all this wealth but to some friend? And how should he know a friend but by trying of him? And how should he try a friend but by troubling of him? And how should he trouble a friend but by borrowing money of him? Now, gentlemen, it may be he'll make his case poor and pitiful to you.

FOSTER: Only to try us?

CLOWN: Only to try you. Do you think we have need of money? Has either of you occasion to use a hundred pound? Need of money, forsooth! As I said afore, only to try you. He has done the like to four or five that I know. You have wits, brains; if he makes his case known to you lay it on. If I said, lay it on, lay it on.

FOSTER: Enough, I understand thee. Master Philip, will you use my aid?

GOODWIN: Or mine?

PHILIP: Worthy friends, to speak freely, as you are gentlemen and I from my childhood have protested love for you, help

with your plenty, to relieve my wants. You know my labour
and have seen my need. Then take some pity on my poor
estate and help to ransom me from slavery by lending me
money.

CLOWN (*aside to* FOSTER *and* GOODWIN): Did I not tell you
so? Lay it on.

FOSTER: Sir, you shall have a hundred pound of me.

GOODWIN: What, need you use him and I so near?

CLOWN: Take it, master, take it.

PHILIP: Where slept this friendship all this while?

CLOWN: Alas, sir, you see their kindness. I told you how
strange he'd take it. Lay it on.

FOSTER: Pray, sir, accept my offer.

GOODWIN: Pray take mine.

CLOWN: Pray, master, accept their courtesies.

PHILIP: I'll use them all, and only borrow thirty pounds
apiece.

CLOWN: Now lay it on.

FOSTER: Take it all of me.

GOODWIN: Why all of you, sir? Is not mine as ready?

FOSTER: When one can do it, why need you trouble two?
But for the thousand pound, sir, do not doubt but you may
trust me with the whole employment of all such moneys.

PHILIP: What thousand pounds?

GOODWIN: Though it be six thousand I durst be steward of
so great a sum.

PHILIP: Do you mock me, gentlemen? My wealth amounts
not to a thousand straws.

CLOWN: Lay it on.

FOSTER: Make not your wealth so dainty, for we know you
have at least six thousand pounds in bank.

PHILIP: Who hath deceived you, derided me, and made a
mockery of my poor estate? Now I protest, I have not in the
world more riches than these garments on my back.

GOODWIN: Is't possible? Why here's my talesman.

CLOWN: The truth is, gentlemen, we have betwixt us no
more than you see.

PHILIP: Only the sixty pounds, promised by you unurged,
may raise my ruined fortunes.

GOODWIN (*to* FOSTER): Will you disburse it all who were
so froward?

FOSTER : I have no money ; you do it for me.

GOODWIN : 'Tis but one man's labour ; do it yourself. If you've no money I have less. God be with you. One stays for me at home.

PHILIP : Why, gentlemen, will you revoke your words? But now you strived which man should lend me most.

FOSTER : But then we reckoned, sir, without our host. (*Both bow and exeunt.*)

PHILIP : Though I be poor, Heaven may yet enable me.
(*Exit.*)

Enter PURSEVANT *and crowd meeting* CLOWN.

PURSEVANT : Whither away so fast, sirrah? In the Queen's name, I command you stay.

CLOWN : What are you that look so big?

PURSEVANT : A pursevant.

CLOWN : If you be pursy can you lend us any money, else tell me the reason why you stay my way?

PURSEVANT : Sirrah, I have a proclamation to publish and because myself am somewhat hoarse, and thou hast a large wide mouth and laudable voice, I charge thee, for the better understanding of the multitude, to speak after me word by word.

CLOWN : I'll speak high enough ; teach me my lesson.

PURSEVANT : Whereas two famous rovers on the sea —

CLOWN : Whereas two famous rogues upon the sea.

PURSEVANT : Purser and Clinton, long since proclaimed pirates —

CLOWN : Long since became spirates —

PURSEVANT : Notwithstanding her Majesty's commission —

CLOWN : Notwithstanding her Majesty's condition —

PURSEVANT : Still keep out —

CLOWN : And will not come in —

PURSEVANT : Therefore I in her Majesty's name —

CLOWN : In her Majesty's name —

PURSEVANT : Proclaim to them or him that can bring in these pirates —

CLOWN : That can bring in these Piecrusts —

PURSEVANT : If a banished man, his country ; if a condemned man, his liberty —

CLOWN: A man at liberty condemned —
PURSEVANT: Besides her Majesty's special favor —
CLOWN: Besides her Majesty's spectacles and favor —
PURSEVANT: And so, God save the Queen.
CLOWN: Have you done, sir?
PURSEVANT: I have — farewell.

(Exit, followed by crowd.)

CLOWN *(holding his head)*: He hath so filled my head with proclamations.

(Exit.)

SCENE 3.—*Interior of* MR. HARDING'S *house.*

MR. HARDING *seated by table.* JOHN *and* WILLIAM *standing near by;* ANN *seated working.*

MR. HARDING: Now, boys, no question but you think it long till I have my state made over to your use.
JOHN: Oh, Lord, sir.
MR. HARDING: To have your eldest brother quite disabled of any inheritance.
WILL: We think it not long, sir, but if you should use all expedition possible, I should say beshrew their hearts that would hinder it. We do not wish our brother disinherited, but, if it be your pleasure, Heaven forbid that we, being your sons, should any way contradict it.
JOHN: We should not show ourselves obedient sons to persuade you to infringe your former vow. For, father, if you remember, you swore long since to do it and Heaven forbid you should break your oath.
MR. HARDING: Lads of my own condition, my own humour! Call me a scrivner, reach me pen and ink, I'll do it immediately.
WILL: Run for a scrivner, Jack.
JOHN: Meantime post thou for pen and ink.

(Exeunt.)

ANN *(rising and going to* MR. HARDING, *stands by his chair putting her arm around his neck)*: Stay, there's no such haste, sweet husband. There be fitter times than these for such affairs. There's no enforcement to make your will, being in such perfect health. Pray if you love me do not talk of death;

besides this expedition in your sons shows that they covet more your lands than life. Defer it then somewhat longer for my sake. (*Kisses him.*)

Mr. HARDING: Then for thy sake I will delay a little, though not long. When heard you from your brother? How falls out his voyage, can you tell?

ANN: I had a letter from him some days since, in which he writes me, all his goods are shipped and nothing wants save a fair gale to bring him to the Straits.

Mr. HARDING: Heaven make his voyage prosperous, for thou knowest I have ventured five hundred pounds with him. If he succeeds it falls out well with me; if not I'm like to share a heavy loss.

Enter WILLIAM, JOHN, GOODWIN *and* FOSTER, PHILIP *and* SUSAN *who set forth a table.*

Mr. HARDING: You are welcome, gentlemen, this day I do entreat you, after the table's ended, to be witness unto some deeds that must inherit these (*indicating* JOHN *and* WILL), and him that is my eldest son quite disable, to which I must entreat your friendly hands.

FOSTER: Mine is at your service.

GOODWIN: So is mine, sir.

WILL: Oh, day long looked for.

JOHN: Now shall we live like two young emperors. Oh, day worthy to be writ in the almanac in red letters for a most famous holiday.

PHILIP: Well, jest on, gentlemen, when all is tried I hope my patience shall exceed your pride.

Mr. HARDING: Come, take your places as your degrees are. Wife, the chair is yours. My loving boys, sit. Let the servants wait.

WILL: Phil, wait at my elbow with a clean trencher; do your duty; you know your place; be ready with a glass of beer, and when I say "fill," fill.

Enter CLOWN.

CLOWN: If please your worship, here is a manner, a kind of sea fowl, desires to have some conference with you.

Mr. HARDING: A sea fowl?

CLOWN : Yes, a sea gull, I mean a mariner; he says he has some news to tell you from my mistress' brother at sea.

MR. HARDING : Touching my venture — prithee, guide him in.

CLOWN : He smells of pitch and tar; if you'll have him to perfume the room I'll show him the way instantly.

MR. HARDING : I prithee, do, and that with expedition.

ANN : I did not look thus soon to hear from him.

MR. HARDING : I fear some strange mishap hath late befallen him.

Enter CLOWN *with* SAILOR.

ANN : Now, honest friend, the news. How fares my brother?

MR. HARDING : How doth my venture prosper?

SAILOR : Sir, your ship is taken; all your goods by pirates seized, your brother prisoner, and of all your venture not the value of one penny saved.

MR. HARDING : That news hath pierced my soul and entered me quite through my heart. I am on the sudden sick, I fear a mortal malady. Oh! oh!

JOHN : How is it with my father? (*All have gathered round to help him.*)

MR. HARDING : Worse! worse! the news of such a great and weighty loss kills all my vitals.

WILL : Father — for Heaven's sake, father, die not yet before you have made over your land.

MR. HARDING : Trouble me not. If I survive this night, you two shall be my heirs.

WILL : This night, if it be thy will.

ANN : Alas, how fare you, sir?

MR. HARDING : Lead me hence and bear me to my bed. My strength doth fail; I cannot help myself.

WILL : Run, run for the writings; they are ready drawn at the scrivner's; bid him bring them quickly, with a vengeance.

MR. HARDING : Let them alone; my hand hath not the strength to guide the pen. Let them alone, I say. Support me to my bed and, my kind neighbours, assist me with your prayers.

(*Exit helped by* PHILIP, SUSAN *and* ANN.)

JOHN: Marry, can he find no time to die but now. Come, let's in.

(*Exeunt.*)

FOSTER: 'Tis strange the bare report of such a loss should strike a man so deeply to the heart.

GOODWIN: I oft have read the like; how some have died with sudden joy, some with exceeding grief.

FOSTER: If he should die intestate, all the land falls to the elder brother; the younger having nothing save from his courtesy.

GOODWIN: I know it; neither lands nor movables. Come, let's hear what further news.

Enter CLOWN.

CLOWN: Oh, my master, what shall I do for my poor master? Never did hard hearted wretch part out of the world so like a lamb. Alas, my poor extortionate master! Many a poor widow hast thou turned into the street and many an orphan made beg their bread. Oh, my sweet, vile, kind, flinty, mild, uncharitable master, he's dead, he's dead. (*Weeps.*)

FOSTER: Dead!

GOODWIN: For the eldest son it happens well.

Enter JACK *and* WILL.

WILL: Jack!

JACK: Will!

WILL: Father's gone!

JACK: So has the land.

WILL: Who shall fill the glass now and wait upon the trenchers?

JACK: Nay, who must go to plough, rub the horse heels, indeed, who must do all the drudgery about the house?

WILL: Could he find no time to die but now? I could cry with anger.

Enter PHILIP, SUSAN *and* ANN.

ANN: Alas for my dear husband!

PHILIP: Comfort yourself; although he die intestate it shall not hurt you who were ever kind to us. How now, brothers, do you weep? I grieve I have lost a father, she a husband.

You lamenting stand not for a father's loss but loss of land. Do you remember with what base contempt you have despised me and my dear loved wife?

JACK: We partly remember it.

PHILIP: So do not I, I have forgot it quite. Though, had you got my lands, Heaven knows how ill you would have dealt with me. Your place if you please is at my table, or where you please if you refuse my kindness.

JACK: This is more of your courtesy than we deserve.

WILL: To trouble your table, there being so many ordinaries in town, were superfluous. Come, Jack.

JACK: Farewell, brother.

CLOWN: Farewell, young masters. (*Kicks them out.*)

PHILIP: And now my friends, who cannot bear the very name of want —

CLOWN: You see we have found the mine.

PHILIP: God be with you henceforth howe'er you speed.

CLOWN (*bowing out* FOSTER *and* GOODWIN): One threescore pound will do it.

PHILIP: Dear mother, the third of all my father's lands are yours and whatever else you like. And now, sweet Sue, it glads me I shall make thee partner of all this plenty.

SUSAN: You are all my wealth. O! would that these fortunes raise my downcast father or recall my banished brother.

PHILIP: All that I have is theirs, but come to my father's burial, whom though his life brought sorrow we cannot .but with funeral tears lament.

(*Exeunt.*)

CLOWN: And now no fellows unless it be at football.

CURTAIN.

ACT V.

SCENE 1.— *Prison drop.*

Enter SHERIFF *leading* PURSER *and* CLINTON *to execution.*

PURSER : How is it with thee, Clinton ?

CLINTON : Well, well.

PURSER : But was it not better when we reigned as lords, nay, kings, at sea ? Those were days.

CLINTON : Yes, golden days, but now our last has come and we must sleep in darkness.

PURSER : Worthy mate, we have a flash left of some half hour long ; that let us burn out bravely. Leave not behind us a snuff of cowardice in the nostrils of our noble countrymen. (*To* SHERIFF) Is our ship well tackled ?

CLINTON : What star must we sail by ? Or what compass ?

SHERIFF (*showing rope*) : I know not the star but here's your compass.

PURSER : Yes, that way points the needle, plague on the pilot.

CLINTON : Hear you, Mr. Sheriff, you see we wear good clothes ; they are paid for and our own ; then give us leave to distribute our own amongst our friends. (*Takes off velvet cape*) There's, sir, for you.

PURSER : The workman that made them ne'er took measure on a hangman's back. Wear this for my sake. (*Gives hat.*)

SHERIFF : Thank your worships.

CLINTON : I wish your knaveship was in our worships' place.

(*Exeunt.*)

SCENE 2.— MR. HARDING'S *Garden.*

Enter ANN.

ANN : Heaven being just could not deal longer roughly with one so virtuous. Philip merits all he hath, but I am doubly unfortunate ; I have lost a husband and a brother too.

MERCHANT (*who has entered during last part of speech*) : A husband, sister, but that brother lives. (*Embraces her.*)

ANN: Can it be so?

MERCHANT: You are the cause I live.

ANN: I, brother, how? Tidings were brought this place your ship was seized * and you a prisoner.

MERCHANT: And 'twas true, yet all these losses I regained by you.

ANN: By me?

MERCHANT: Thus it was. You saved the life of a young gentleman whom for your sake I furnished out to sea. He, when my ship was taken and I surprised, by valiant fight re-captured and restored my fortune, and made me sharer of the rich pirates' prize.

ANN: That gentleman?

MERCHANT: The self same. I have a further token of his gratitude. In this choice jewel he commends to you millions of gratulations and kind thanks. To his sister this sum of gold to redeem her wretched husband and herself from a slavery which now I see death hath done for them.

ANN: These tokens will be joyful to them both, but more welcome the tidings of his safety. We do wrong to keep news of such joy so long from them. Let's in.

(*Exeunt into house.*)

Enter OLD *and* YOUNG FORREST *well dressed.*

OLD FORREST: A father's blessing more than all thy honours crowns thee. Besides thy pardon and thy country's freedom, what favours hath her grace conferred on thee?

FORREST: She hath styled me with the order of knighthood and promise of employment of more weight for the service of my country. And now I must visit that fair gentlewoman to whom I stand indebted for my life.

OLD FORREST: A grateful friend thou art, a kind dear brother and a most loving son.

Enter PHILIP, SUSAN, MERCHANT *and* ANN.

PHILIP: Sir, more than all these fortunes late befallen me, my noble brother's late business at sea hath filled me with most joy.

* Original "spoiled."

ANN: Of his goodness we have had sufficient taste already but his presence would complete our happiness.

SUSAN: That would seem like surfeit after sweetmeats.

FORREST: See, all my friends, but first let me salute her to whom I am most bound. (*Kisses* ANN'S *hand.*)

SUSAN (*running to her father*): My most dear father.

ANN: You are grateful, sir, much beyond my merit.

SUSAN: Oh, spare me, sir, to fly into his arms that hath so long fled from me.

FORREST (*embracing her*): My sweet sister.

PHILIP: I am one among the rest that love you.

MERCHANT: And I though last in my acknowledgment am first in due arrearage.

FORREST: My friend, to whom, next to your sister, I stand most engaged for a forfeit life! And now, fair lady, I dare more boldly look upon your face than when I saw you last. On whom can I better confer my fortunes and myself than her to whom I owe my life? Be then to me what I have styled you last, my lady.

MERCHANT: You are not my sister if you deny him.

PHILIP: Let me plead for him.

SUSAN: O doubly link me to you!

FORREST: Sweet, your answer?

ANN: Sir, I should much mistake my own fair ends, should I alone withstand so many friends. I am yours and only yours.

FORREST: I yours the same, and now I kiss you by that name.

Enter CLOWN *and a crowd of people, including* BESS.

CLOWN: What, kissing already? I smell another wedding. Good sir, here's a maid would speak with you.

MERCHANT: With me! what, Bess?

BESS: I bring you, sir, the bag of gold you bade me guard till your return.

MERCHANT: Keep it, fair maid, for a wedding dower.

CLOWN: If it please you, sir, I'll take it and her too.

FORREST: Dear lady, sister, friend, nay, brother too, and you, sir, most endeared! In us the world may see our fates well scanned. Fortune in me by sea, in you by land.

FINIS.

FORTUNE BY LAND AND SEA

A Tragi-Comedy

BY

THOMAS HEYWOOD
&
WILLIAM ROWLEY

EDITED BY

BARRON FIELD, Esq.

For the SHAKESPEARE
SOCIETY, LONDON
1845

THE PERSONS OF THE PLAY.

OLD FORREST.
FRANK FORREST, } his sons.
YOUNG FORREST, }
OLD HARDING.
PHILIP, his eldest son, married to SUSAN FORREST.
WILLIAM, } his younger sons.
JOHN, }
MASTER RAINSFORD, a quarrelsome Gentleman.
GOODWIN, } Friends to Rainsford.
FOSTER, }
A MERCHANT, brother to MRS. HARDING.
PURSER, } Pirates.
CLINTON, }
CLOWN.
PURSUIVANT.
HOST.
SAILORS.
HANGMAN.
DRAWERS.
OFFICERS.
MRS. ANNE HARDING, second wife to OLD HARDING.
SUSAN, daughter of OLD FORREST, wife to PHILIP HARDING.

The SCENE, London, (and on the Sea).

FORTUNE BY LAND AND SEA.

ACT I.

SCENE I.—*Old Forrest's House.*

Enter RAINSFORD, OLD FORREST FRANK FORREST, SUSAN FORREST, GOODWIN, *and* FOSTER.

RAINS. I prithee, Frank, let's have thy company to supper.

FRANK. With all my heart: if I can but give my father here the slip by six o'clock, I will not fail.

RAINS. I'll talk with him. I prithee, old man, lend us thy son to-night. We'll borrow him but for some two hours, and send him home again to thee presently.

GOOD. Faith, do, Mr. Forrest; he cannot spend his time in better company.

OLD FOR. Oh, gentlemen, this too much liberty
Breeds many strange outrageous ills in youth,
And fashions them to vice.

RAINS. Nay, school us not, old man. Some of us are too old to learn; and being past whipping too, there's no hope of profiting. If we shall have him, say so. If not, I prithee keep him still, and God give thee good of him!

FRANK. Nay, will you be gone? I'll be at the heels of you, as I live.

FOS. 'Tis enough. Nay, come; and if we shall go, let us go.

OLD FOR. Nay, gentlemen, do not mistake me, pray.
I love my son, but do not doat on him;
Nor is he such a darling in my eye,
That I am loath to have him from my sight.
Yet let me tell you, had you, gentlemen,
Call'd him to any fairer exercise,
As practice of known weapons, or to back

Some gallant gennet; had it been to dance,
Leap in the fields, to wrestle, or to try
Masteries in any noble quality,
I could have spared him to you half his age;
But call him out to drinking, of all skill,
I hold that much-us'd practice the most ill.

    Frank.   I told him you would still be urging him, and see what comes on't?

    Rains.   Sir, what we do's in love, and let you know,
We do not need his purse nor his acquaintance,
Nor, if you should mistake, can we be sorry,
Nor wound to ask your pardon.   Fare ye well!
Come, gentlemen.

               (*Exeunt* Rainsford, Goodwin, *and* Foster.)

    Frank.   Will you be gone? I'll come.

    Old For.   Oh, son! that thou wilt follow rioting,
Surfeit by drinking and unseasoned hours!
These gentlemen perhaps may do't; they're rich,
Well-landed, and their fathers purchase daily,
Where I, Heav'n knows, the world still frowning on me,
Am forc'd to sell and mortgage to keep you.
His brother ranks himself with the best gallants
That flourish in the kingdom: though not able
To spend with them, yet, for his virtuous parts,
He is borne out, his person woo'd and sought,
And they more bound to him for his discourse,
Than he to them for their expense and cost.
Thy course is otherwise; will drinking healths,
Cups of mull'd sack, and glasses elbow deep,
Drunk in thy youth, maintain thee in thine age?
No, 'twill not hold out, boy.

      Frank.   My company hath not been to your purse so
           chargeable.
I do not spend so much.

      Old For.   Thou spend'st thy time.
More precious than thy coin, consum'st thy hopes,
In drowning surfeits. Tell me, canst thou call
That thrift, to be in all these prodigal?
Use thy discretion; somewhat I divine;
Mine is the care, the loss or profit thine.

                       (*Exit.*)

SUSAN. Brother, be ruled. My father grieves to see you given to these boundless riots. Will you follow?

FRANK. Lead you the way, I'll after you.

SUSAN. 'Tis well; we'll look for you within.

FRANK. When? Can you tell?

(*Exeunt severally.*)

SCENE 2.— *A Tavern.*

Enter RAINSFORD, GOODWIN, *and* FOSTER.

RAINS. Boy, my cloak.

Enter A DRAWER.

GOOD. Our cloaks, sirrah!

FOS. Why, drawer!

DRAW. Here, sir.

RAINS. Some canary sack, and tobacco.

DRAW. You shall, sir. Wilt please you stay supper?

RAINS. Yes, marry, will we, sir: let's have the best cheer the kitchen yields. The pipe, sirrah!

DRAW. Here, sir.

RAINS. Will Frank be here at supper?

GOOD. So, sir, he promised, and presumes he will not fail his hour.

RAINS. Some sack, boy! I am all lead within. There's no mirth in me; nor was I wont to be so lumpish sad. Reach me the glass. What's this?

DRAW. Good sherry sack, sir.

RAINS. I meant canary, sir. What? hast no brains? (*Strikes him.*)

DRAW. Pox o' your brains! Are your fingers so light?

RAINS. Say, sir?

DRAW. You shall have canary presently.

GOOD. When was he wont to be in this sad strain? Excepting some few sudden melancholies, there lives not one more free and sociable.

FOS. I am too well acquainted with his humour, to stir his blood in the least distemperature. Coz, I'll be with you here.

Re-enter DRAWER.

RAINS. Do, come to me. Have you hit upon the right canary now? or could your hog's head find a Spanish butt? A health.

GOOD. Were it my height, I'll pledge it.

FOS. How do you now, man?

RAINS. Well, well, exceeding well; my melancholy sadness steals away, and, by degrees, shrinks from my troubled heart. Come, let's be merry. More tobacco, boy; and bring in supper.

Enter FRANK.

FOS. Welcome! welcome! Wilt thou be here, old lad?

GOOD. Or here?

FRANK. Wherefore hath Nature lent me two hands, but to use them both at once? My cloak. I am for you here and here.

FOS. Bid them make haste of supper. Some discourse, to pass away the time.

RAINS. Now, Frank, how stole you from your father's arms? You have been schooled, no doubt: fie, fie upon't.
Ere I would live in such base servitude
To an old gray beard, 'sfoot, I'd hang myself.
A man cannot be merry and drink drunk,
But he must be controll'd by gravity.

FOR. O pardon him! you know he is my father,
And what he doth is but paternal love.
Tho' I be wild, I am not so past reason,
His person to despise, though I his counsel
Cannot severely follow.

RAINS. 'Sfoot, he's a fool.

FRANK. A fool! y're a —

FOS. Nay, gentlemen.

FRANK. Yet I restrain my tongue,
Hoping you speak out of some spleenful rashness,
And no deliberate malice; and it may be
You are sorry that a word so unreverent,
To wrong so good an aged gentleman,
Should pass you unawares.

RAINS. Sorry, sir boy. You will not take exceptions?

FRANK. Not against you with willingness, whom I have

loved so long. Yet you might think me a most dutiless and ungracious son, to give smooth countenance unto my father's wrong. Come, I dare swear 'twas not your malice; and I take it so. Let's frame some other talk. Hear, gentlemen.

RAINS. But hear me, boy: it seems, sir, you are angry.

FRANK. Not thoroughly yet.

RAINS. Then what would anger thee?

FRANK. Nothing from you.

RAINS. Of all things under heaven,
What would'st thou loathest have me do?

FRANK. I would not have you wrong my reverend father, and I hope you will not.

RAINS. Thy father's an old dotard.

FRANK. I could not brook this at a monarch's hands;
Much less at thine.

RAINS. Ay, boy! then take you that. (*Flings wine in his face.*)

FRANK. I was not born to brook this. (*They fight.*)
Oh! I am slain. (*Dies.*)

GOOD. Sweet coz, what have you done! Shift for yourself.

RAINS. Away!

(*Exeunt.*)

Enter TWO DRAWERS.

1 DRAW. Stay the gentlemen: they have killed a man.
Oh, sweet Mr. Francis! One run to his father's.

2 DRAW. Had not we drawers enough in the house, but they must needs draw too?

1 DRAW. They have drawn blood of this gentleman, that I have drawn many a quart of wine to. Oh, sweet Mr. Francis. Hark, hark! I hear his father's voice below. Ten to one he is come to fetch him home to supper: and now he may carry him home to his grave. See, here he comes.

Enter the HOST, OLD FORREST, *and* SUSAN.

HOST. You must take comfort, sir.

OLD FOR. Would Heaven I could; or that I might beg patience.

SUS. Oh my brother!

OLD FOR. Is he dead, is he dead, girl?

Sus. Aye, dead, sir : Frank is dead.

Old For.   Alas, alas ! my boy ! I have not the heart
To look upon his wide and gaping wounds.
Hide them, oh, hide them from me, lest those mouths
Through which his life past through do swallow mine.
Pray tell me, sir, doth this appear to you
Fearful and pitiful, to you that are
A stranger to my dead boy ?

Host.   How can it be otherwise ?

Old For.   Oh, me, most wretched of all wretched men !
If to a stranger his warm bleeding wounds
Appear so grisly and so lamentable,
How will they seem to me, who am his father ?
Will they not hale my eyeballs from their rounds,
And with an everlasting blindness strike them ?

Sus. Oh, sir, look here !

Old For.   Dost long to have me blind ?
Then I'll behold them since I know thy mind.
Oh, me, is this my son that doth so senseless lie,
And swims in blood ? my soul with his shall fly
Unto the land of rest.   Behold I crave,
Being kill'd with grief, we both may have one grave.

Sus.   Alas, my father's dead too ! Gentle sir,
Help to retire his spirits, overtravailed
With age and sorrow.

Host.   Mr. Forrest !

Sus.   Father !

Old For.   What says my girl ? good morrow.   What's
    o'clock ?
That you are up so early ?   Call up Frank.
Tell him he lies too long abed this morning.
'Was wont to call the sun up and to raise
The early lark, and mount her 'mongst the clouds.
Will he not up ? rise, rise, thou sluggish boy.

Sus.   Alas ! he cannot, father.

Old For.   Cannot.   Why?

Sus.   Do you not see his bloodless colour fail ?

Old For.   Perhaps he's sickly that he looks so pale ?

Sus.   Do you not feel his pulse no motion keep ?
How still he lies !

OLD FOR. Then is he fast asleep.

SUS. Do you not see his fatal eyelid close?

OLD FOR. Speak softly. Hinder not his soft repose.

SUS. Oh, see you not these purple conduits run?
Know you these wounds?

OLD FOR. Oh, me! my murder'd son!

Enter YOUNG FORREST.

YOUNG FOR. Sister!

SUS. Oh, brother, brother!

YOUNG FOR. Father, how cheer you, sir? why, you were
wont to store for others' comfort, that by sorrow were any way
distrest. Have you all wasted, and spared none to yourself?

OLD FOR. Oh, son, son, son! see, alas, see where thy
brother lies. He dined with me to-day, was merry. Merry, ay,
that corpse was, he that lies here. See, there thy murdered
brother and my son was. See, dost thou not weep for him?

YOUNG FOR. I shall find time.
When you have took some comfort, I'll begin
To mourn his death, and scourge the murderer's sin.
Dear father, be advis'd; take hence his body,
And let it have a solemn funeral.

OLD FOR. But for the murd'rer, shall not he attend
The sentence of the law with all severity?

YOUNG FOR. Have you but patience. Should we urge the
        law,
He hath such honourable friends to guard him,
We should in that but bark against the moon.
Nay, do not look that way: take hence the body,
Let the law sleep: the time ere it be long,
May offer't self to a more just revenge.
We're poor, and the world frowns on all our fortune.
With patience then bear this amongst the rest.
The Heav'ns, when they be pleas'd, may turn the wheel
Of Fortune round, when we, that are dejected,
May be again rais'd to our former height.

OLD FOR. Oh, when saw father such a tragic sight,
And did outlive it? never, son, ah, never
From mortal breast ran such a precious river.

YOUNG FOR.   Come, father, and dear sister, join with me.
Let us all learn our sorrows to forget;
He ow'd a death, and he hath paid that debt.

(Exeunt.)

SCENE 3.— OLD HARDING'S House.

Enter OLD HARDING, his two sons, WILLIAM and JOHN, and his wife
ANNE, as newly come from the wedding.

OLD HAR.   So, things are as they should be.   We have attained
The height of solace and true joy, sweet Nan.
No sooner married but a mother of this
My hopeful issue.   Cheer thy thoughts,
For what I want in youth, I will supply
In true affection ; and what age doth scant me
In sprightly vigour, I'll make good in wealth.

MRS. HAR.   Sir, you well know, I was not easily won,
And therefore not soon changed.   Advisedly,
Not rashly, did I venture on your love.
My young unsettled thoughts, from their long travels,
Have late attained unto their journey's end,
And they are now at rest.

OLD HAR.   Here they have found a harbour to retire to.

WILL.   'Twould become you to use my father here respectively : you see how he receives you almost dowerless.

JOHN.   True, where he, out of his own abilities, might have
commanded widows richer far, ay, and perhaps each way as
beautiful.

MRS. H.   Upbraid me not.   I do confess he might,
Nor was this match my seeking.   If't hath pleased
Your father, for some virtues known in me,
To grace me with his free election,
Methinks it worse becomes you, being sons,
To blame a father's pleasure.   Howsoever,
Better myself I cannot.   If he thought me
Worthy his bed, I see small reason you
Should wrong me to him, that my state best knew.

OLD HAR.   Nan, I am pleas'd : they shall be satisfied ;
And, boys, I tell you, tho' you be my sons,

You much forget your duty to a mother,
Whom I hold worthy to be called my wife.
No more of this, I charge you.

WILL. Sir, we've done.

OLD HAR. No child to her, can be to me no son.

JOHN. I am pleased : here my spleen dies,
Suddenly fallen, as it did quickly rise.

OLD HAR. This is the end I aim'd at. Were my eldest
Present among us much, I had my height
Of wishes.

Enter CLOWN.

CLOWN. I have been there, sir.

OLD HAR. And foundest thou my son Philip?

CLOWN. When you had given him me in charge, I had of
him great care. I have took of him great care; and I have
took him napping, as you know who took his mare. I found
your son Philip, like a cock-sparrow billing. If I had staid but
a little longer, I might have taken him and his hen treading.
I know not whether it be St. Valentine's day or no; but I am ·
sure they are coupled. ·

OLD HAR. How coupled, dost thou mean?

CLOWN. I see them one and one, and that you know makes
two, and two makes a couple; and they, well coupled, may in
time make a third between them. I do not think but 'tis like
to be a match.

OLD HAR. I vow, if e'er he match into that family,
The kindred be'ng all beggar'd, that forc'd union
Shall make a firm divorce 'twixt him and mine.

Enter PHILIP *and* SUSAN.

CLOWN. Here they are, sir, coram nobis. You will find it
a plain case, if the matter be well searched. I have spoke but
what I have seen; and now let every one answer for themselves.

OLD HAR. What mean these hands?

PHIL. Nothing, sir,
Save a mere interchange of hearts and souls,
Doubly made fast by vows.

OLD HAR. 'Twixt her and thee?

PHIL.   So, and no otherwise.

OLD HAR.   Yet thou hast time
To pause and to repent; but after this,
No limit to consider; cast her off,
Or henceforth I disclaim thee for my son.

PHIL.   Yet I shall ever hold you for my father.

OLD HAR.   Then show in this thy duty : quite forsake her,
And be restor'd into my family.

PHIL.   O, sir, she is a virgin chaste and fair,
Unto whose bed I am by oath engaged.
That power above, that heard the contract pass,
Both heard, approv'd, and still records the same.
Oh, sir, I am of years : oft have you wished
To see me well bestow'd ; and now's the time
Your wish hath took effect.   It was your prayer
That Heav'ns would send me a good wife; and lo!
In her they have show'd their bounty.

OLD HAR.   Thou thy baseness.
Take one that's of my choosing.

PHIL.   Do men use,
By others' hearts and eyes their wives to choose?

OLD HAR.   She's poor.

PHIL.   Yet virtuous.

OLD HAR.   Virtue! a sweet dower!

PHIL.   Yet that, when Mammon fails, retains her power.

OLD HAR.   Possess'd of virtue then thou need nought else.

PHIL.   Riches may waste by fire, by sea, by stealth,
But water, fire, nor theft can virtue waste.
When all else fails us, that alone shall last.

OLD HAR.   Go to Cheapside, with virtue in your purse,
And cheapen plate; or to the shambles hie,
And see what meat with virtue you can buy.
Will virtue make the pot seeth, or the jack
Turn a spit laden? tell me, will your landlord
At quarter-day take virtue for his rent?
Will your wife's virtue yield you ten in the hundred?
A good stock would do all this.   Come, come, son;
I'll find thee a rich match; and turn her off.

WILL.   'Faith, do, brother.   The only way to thrive is to be
ruled by my father.

JOHN. Do you think I, being but the youngest, would marry under the degree of a gentlewoman; and that without my father's consent too?

PHIL. I wish you may not; but withal advise you,
To make a conscience how you break a vow.
And, sir, for you, with pardon, I could trace you
Even in that path in which I stand condemn'd.
This gentlewoman, my beautous mother-in-law,
(Whose virtues I both honor and admire,
Whom in no kind I envy) I presume,
You married not for riches; for if so,
Where is that wealthy dower she brought along?
Being yourself example, blame me not,
To make a father my strict precedent.
In viewing me, bear but yourself in mind,
And prove to her, as I to this like kind.

MRS. H. The gentleman speaks well. Pray, let me mediate
Between you a reconcilement.

WILL. Good sir, do.

JOHN. Since 'tis my mother's pleasure to take't well,
We'll be joint suitors with her.

CLOWN. And I, too, good master.

OLD HAR. The boy's inflexible, and I obdure.
He cannot be more saucy to object
That which I would not hear, than I perverse
In yielding to a knave so obstinate.

SUS. He is your son, and of your blood the first;
Brand him not with a name so odious.
You cannot write yourself a gentleman,
But leave him of that name inheritor.
Tho' you have power to take away his means,
Deprive him both your blessing and your love,
Which methinks in a father should seem strange,
His state you may, his blood you cannot, change.

OLD HAR. Baited on all sides? have I been thus long
A father and a master to direct,
To be at these years pupil'd by a girl?
A beggar? one that all the wealth she has
Bears on her back; and shall I suffer this?
Whilst these, that ought to arm me with just rage,

Preach to me patience? I'll endure no more.
Come, leave them, sweet wife! Gentle sons away!

(*Exeunt.*)

PHIL. I'll have thee yet, tho' all the world say nay.

(*Exeunt.*)

CLOWN. Now, which of these parties shall I cleave to and follow? Well, now I remember myself, I'll show myself a true citizen, and stick to the stronger side.

(*Exit.*)

SCENE 4.— *The Street.*

Enter RAINSFORD *and* YOUNG FORREST, *meeting.*

YOUNG FOR. Pray, let me speak with you.
RAINS. With me, sir?
YOUNG FOR. With you.
RAINS. Say on.
YOUNG FOR. Do you not know me?
RAINS. Keep off, upon the peril of thy life.
Come not within my sword's length, lest this arm
Prove fatal to thee, and bereave thy life,
As it hath done thy brother's.
YOUNG FOR. Why now thou know'st me truly, by that token,
That thou hast slain my brother. Put up, put up!
So great a quarrel as a brother's life
Must not be made a street-brawl; 'tis not fit
That every prentice should, with his shop club,
Betwixt us play the sticklers. Sheathe thy sword.
RAINS. Swear thou wilt act no sudden violence,
Or this sharp sword shall still be interposed
'Twixt me and thy known hatred.
YOUNG FOR. Sheathe thy sword.
By my religion and that interest
I have in gentry, I will not be guilty
Of any base revenge.
RAINS. Say on.
YOUNG FOR. Let's walk.
Trust me. Let not thy guilty soul
Be jealous of my fury. This my hand.

Is curbed and govern'd by an honest heart,
Not by just anger. I'll not touch thee foully
For all the world. Let's walk.
   RAINS. Proceed.
   YOUNG FOR. Sir, you did kill my brother. Had it been
In fair and even encounter, tho' a child,
His death I had not question'd.
   RAINS. Is this all?
   YOUNG FOR. He's gone. The law is past. Your life is
      clear'd;
For none of all our kindred laid against
You evidence to hang you. You're a gentleman;
And pity 'twere a man of your descent
Should die a felon's death. See, sir, thus far
We have demeaned fairly, like ourselves.
But, think you, though we wink at base revenge,
A brother's death can be so soon forgot?
Our gentry baffled, and our name disgraced?
No: 'tmust not be; I am a gentleman
Well known; and my demeanor hitherto
Hath promis'd somewhat. Should I swallow this,
The scandal would outlive me. Briefly then,
I'll fight with you.
   RAINS. I am loath.
   YOUNG FOR. Answer directly,
Whether you dare to meet me on even terms;
Or mark how I'll proceed.
   RAINS. Say, I deny it.
   YOUNG FOR. Then I say thou'rt a villain, and I challenge
      thee,
Where'er I meet thee next, in field or town,
The father's manors, or thy tenants' grange,
Saving the church, there is no privilege
In all this land for thy despised life.
No guard of friends, no nightwalks, or sly stealth,
No jealous fear, which in a murderer's eye
Keeps hourly watch, shall have the privilege,
This even and balanc'd fight, body to body;
I'll kill thee be it in thy bed, at meat,
In thy wife's arms; as thou tookest my brother,
With thy back towards me, basely. Answer me.

RAINS. I'll meet with thee. The hour?

YOUNG FOR. By six to-morrow morning. 'Tis your privilege

T'appoint the place and weapon.

RAINS. Hounslow the place : my choice of weapon this.
(*Showing his sword.*)

YOUNG FOR. I can except at neither. Fail the place,
Or suit your weapon's length. Farewell !

(*Exit.*)

Enter GOODWIN *and* FOSTER.

GOOD. Now, cousin Rainsford.

RAINS. I'll so swinge my younker.

FOS. Why, who hath rais'd this storm, sir ?

RAINS. Wot'st thou what ?
The younger Forrest parted but ev'n now,
Call'd me to question 'bout his brother's death,
And since hath challenged me.

GOOD. Challeng'd ?

RAINS. Challeng'd me.

FOS. Why, he is too weak for you.

RAINS. Yes, I shall weak him.
My purpose is to teach the stripling sense ;
An' you be honest gentlemen, stand but
Aloof to-morrow, and observe how I
Will swinge my youth about the field.

GOOD. An' please Heav'n, I'll be there.

FOS. And so will I.

RAINS. He seeks his fate. And murd'rers, once being in,
Wade further till they drown. Sin pulls on sin.

(*Exeunt.*)

ACT II.

SCENE 1.— OLD HARDING'S *House*.

Enter OLD HARDING, MRS. HARDING, WILLIAM *and* JOHN.

WILL. 'Tis true, upon my life.

OLD HAR. Say what thou wilt, I'll not believe it, boy.

WILL. Do you believe me to be your son William?

OLD HAR. Well.

WILL. Do you believe I stand here?

OLD HAR. On.

WILL. That this gentlewoman is your wife?

OLD HAR. So.

WILL. That Jack Harding here is my brother?

OLD HAR. Good.

WILL. That I speak to you? that you list to me?
Do you believe anything that is to be believed?

OLD HAR. What of all this?

WILL. Then believe my brother Philip has married Mistress
Susan. I saw them in the church together, I heard them pronounce the words together. Whether it be better, or worse,
for them, I know not, but they are in for better, and worse, that
I am sure.

OLD HAR. As sure as thou art certain this is true,
So sure I'll disinherit the proud boy,
And all the magazine, that I enjoy,
Divide 'tween you, my sons.

JOHN. Not all, father. Alas! allow him some small legacy
to live on.

WILL. If't be but a cast farm, or some poor cottage, rather
than nothing. It may be he'll content himself with a little.
You know something hath a savour.

OLD HAR. He that hath set me and my love at nothing,
I'll leave him worth as little.

MRS. H. Chide him you may, but yet not cast him off;
For fathers ought most chastise where they love.
Parents, as I have read, their rage should hide,
Where children fall through weakness, not through pride.

OLD HAR. They are none such to me. My vow is past ;
My life may fade, but yet my will shall last.

Enter PHILIP *and* SUSAN.

WILL. See, where the four bare legs that belong to a bed
    come.
I could almost pity him.
JOHN. And why pity him? all the while that marriage is
the first step to our making?
PHIL. See, sir, 'tis done.
OLD HAR. And thou undone.
PHIL. In losing your kind favour more undone,
Than in your casual wealth.
OLD HAR. By all that I enjoy —
PHIL. Oh, swear not! spare that oath; I'll credit you,
Altho' you speak but mildly.
OLD HAR. So thrive I, if for this marriage,
Made in despite of me, I make thee partner
Of any substance that's accounted mine.
PHIL. Not made in spite of you. Unsay that language;
And then you chide me truly, as I live:
And tho' on earth by you disherited,
Hope to be heir to heav'n. I match'd with her
In sincere love, but in no spleen to you.
Tho' you have sworn to give my fortunes from me,
You have not sworn to reave me of your love.
That let me have: let others take the land.
OLD HAR. My love goes with my land; and in this marriage
Thou hast lost both.
PHIL. Your substance I despise;
But, to lose that, draws rivers from my eyes.
MRS. H. Oh, bear a soft and more relenting soul,
This gentlewoman's birth.
OLD HAR. Wife! wife! if he have married her for birth,
Then let her birth maintain him.
MRS. H. My kind sons,
Speak to your father.
WILL. Alas! mother, you hear my father hath sworn; and
do you love him, and would make him break his oath?

JOHN. Engage his soul? that were a wife's part indeed!

WILL. As I live, I would not wish him, now he has sworn, to alter his mind in the least circumstance, for more than I'll speak.

PHIL. I am a kinder son than you be brothers.
Have you renounc'd me for your son?

OLD HAR. I have.

JOHN. You see he has.

PHIL. You have not yet renounc'd me for your servant.
That title let me bear. I'll be your man,
And wear your livery; since my poverty
Enforces me to serve, let it be you.

WILL. Grant him that, good father. When you want employment for him, I may sometimes have occasion to use him myself.

JOHN. A reasonable motion. You want a serving-man. Since you must hire one on force, as good him as another.

PHIL. He wants a maid too. Let him hire this woman, his servant, not his daughter. Give us but as you would do to strangers, we are pleased.

WILL. The motion's not amiss. Can you milk, sweetheart?

SUS. I can.

WILL. And sweep a house, serve a hog, grope a hen, feel a duck, wash and wring?

SUS. What I have us'd, my soft hand best can show;
But what I cannot, I'll be glad to learn.

JOHN. A good willing mind in troth. And can you bake and brew?

SUS. I shall be easily taught.

JOHN. You had best look to it; for as you brew, so you are like to drink.

OLD HAR. Sirrah, sirrah! Can you hold the plough, and thresh, sow, reap, load a cart, drive a team?

PHIL. These, or what else, I'll practise.

OLD HAR. Come, then, off with these gay clothes, no habits fit for hinds. Help, boys, to suit them as their fortunes are. Go, search in the clown's wardrobe.

WILL. Fear not. We'll fit 'em as well as if we had ta'en measure of them.

MRS. H. To see this misery with patience borne,
Makes me to pity where these others scorn.

JOHN. Here, sir, is that will serve the turn. If you employ him in the cornfields, I'll warrant him fright the birds. Here's that will make him look like a scarecrow.

WILL. And here's that will change the copy of her case, though not of her countenance.

OLD HAR. Too good for drudges. Live now by your sweat, And at your labour make account to eat.

PHIL. Here's but a sorry wedding-day!

SUS. My sweet Philip,
That thou should'st suffer these extremes for me,
Only for me!

PHIL. Let that, betwixt my soul
And thine, be witness of my constant love.
Alas, for thee! that thou must drudge and toil,
And having been a mistress all thy life,
Must now become a servant.

Enter CLOWN.

CLOWN. This being the wedding-day of my master's eldest son, I expect rare cheer; as, first, the great spiced cake to go in, cake-bread fashion, drawn out with currants: the jealous furmety must put on his yellow hose again, and hot pies come mincing after: the boiled mutton must swim in a river of stewed broth, where the channel is made of prunes, instead of pebbles, and prime raisins and currants in the stead of checker-stones and gravel; to omit geese and gulls, ducks and dotterels, widgeons and woodcocks, of which there will be plenty. At our wedding dinner we shall have the bride, in her tiffety-taffeties most sumptuous, and the bridegroom as well, in branched satin, as branched rosemary, most coura-geous. I'll in and see them in all their beauty, and give them the joy, the bon-jour, the besilasmanos, or, to be more vulgar to the incapable, the God give you good morrow.

PHIL. Good morrow, fellow Simkin!

CLOWN. 'Tis he: no, no, 'tis not he.

SUS. Good Simkin.

CLOWN. Her face! the trick of her eye, her leer, her blink, her askew! but to say it is she, Proh deum atque hominum fidem!

PHIL. Art thou amaz'd to see me thus transform'd,
Or thus altered? None but such a father,
Such a remorseless and hard-hearted father,
Could so translate his children.

CLOWN. Oh, Mr. Philip! I see your father is no scholar,
but a mere dunce. I protest I never read a more vile transla-
tion.

SUS. Nor saw so sudden and unmeet a change.

CLOWN. Oh, young mistress! Ovid's Metamorphoses could
never show the like. But how comes this to pass? the manner? the manner? my heart begins to condole, and my con-
duit-pipes to open. We shall have a shower presently. The
manner?

PHIL. This morning, having married my betrothed,
For could I less do, having vow'd so much?
I came to him, and most submissively entreated
Pardon for myself and her.

CLOWN. Kind young man! hold, good heart!

PHIL. He presently reviles us; then renounc'd us;
Nor would he give us, should he see us starve,
And famish at his gate, no, not a crust
Of his hinds' bread; or of his smallest beer,
Not a bare cruseful, should we die of thirst.

CLOWN. 'Twill out! 'Twill out! but now for the apparel.

SUS. When he renounc'd us for his children,
We had no means reserv'd unless with baseness
To beg our victuals; were resolv'd to work;
So he at our entreaty, hir'd us both
To be his hinds·and drudges.

CLOWN. Your apron, good mistress! And so and so, you
were stript out of your silks and satins, and forced to put on
these russets and sheepskins.

PHIL. Even so.

CLOWN. O, most tyrannical old fornicator — old master, I
would say. Well, since 'tis so, no more young master, but
fellow servant; no more master Philip, but Phil; here's my
hand; I'll do two men's labours in one, to save you a labour;
and, to spare your shoulders, I'll help at many a dead lift.
Come, I'll go teach you hayt and ree, gee and whoe, and which
is to which hand. Next, I'll learn you the names of all our

team, and acquaint you with Jock, the fore-horse, and Fib, the fill-horse, and with all the god-a-mercy fraternity.

Sus.　Succeed it as Heav'n please !

Phil.　What must be must be : Heav'n hath set it down :
At what they smile, why should we mortals frown ?

Clown.　To see so brave a gentleman turn clown !

(Exeunt.)

Scene 2.— *Hounslow.*

Enter Goodwin *and* Foster.

Fos.　Are we not somewhat too early, think you ?

Good.　It appears so, for neither challenger nor defendant are yet in the field.

Fos.　Which way do you think the day will go ? or whether of them do you hold to be the better man ?

Good.　That I am not able to judge ; but if the opinion of the world hold current, he that killed one brother, it is thought will be the death of the other. But these things are beyond us. Lie close, for being seen.

Enter Rainsford *and* Young Forrest.

Rains.　Your resolution, holds then ?

Young For.　Men that are easily mov'd are soon remov'd
From resolution ; but when, with advice
And with foresight we purpose, our intents
Are not without considerate reasons alter'd.

Rains.　Thou art resolved, and I prepar'd for thee.
Yet thus much know, thy state is desperate,
And thou art now in danger's throat already
Ev'n half-devour'd. If I subdue thee, know
Thou art a dead man ; for this fatal steel,
That searched thy brother's entrails is prepar'd
To do as much to thee. If thou survivest,
And I be slain, th'art dead too ; my alliance
And greatness in the world will not endure
My slaughter unavenged. Come, I am for thee.

Young For.　I would my brother liv'd, that this our diff'rence
Might end in an embrace of folded love ;

But 'twas Heaven's will that for some guilt of his
He should be scourged by thee; and for the guilt
In scourging him, thou by my vengeance punish'd.
Come; I am both ways arm'd, against thy steel
If I be pierc'd by it, or 'gainst thy greatness
If mine pierce thee.

    RAINS. Have at thee. (*They fight and pause.*)

    YOUNG FOR. I will not bid thee hold; but if thy breath
Be as much short as mine, look to thy weakness.

    RAINS. The breath, thou draw'st but weakly,
Thou now shalt draw no more. (*They fight.*— FORREST *loseth*
    his weapon.)

    YOUNG FOR. That Heaven knows.
He guard my body that my spirit owes! (*Guards himself, and*
    puts by with his hat — slips — the other running, falls
    over him and FORREST *kills him.*)

    GOOD. My cousin's fall'n — pursue the murderer.

    FOS. But not too near, I pray; you see he's armed,
And in this deep amazement may commit
Some desperate outrage.

    YOUNG FOR. Had I but known the terror of this deed,
I would have left it done imperfectly,
Rather than in this guilt of conscience
Labour'd so far. But I forget my safety.
The gentleman is dead, my desp'rate life
Will be o'erswayed by his allies and friends,
And I have now no safety but by flight.
And see where my pursuers come. Away!
Certain destruction hovers o'er my stay.

                                   (*Exit.*)

    GOOD. Come, follow! see he takes towards the city.
You bear the body of my cousin hence,
Unto the neighb'ring village. I'll still keep
Within the murder's sight. Raise hue and cry!
He shall not 'scape our pursuit, tho' he fly.

                                   (*Exeunt.*)

SCENE 3.— OLD HARDING'S *Garden.*

Enter WILLIAM *and* PHILIP.

WILL. Now, wilt truss me that point, Philip? I could find in my heart to beg thee of my father to wait upon me: but that I am afraid he cannot spare thee from the plough. Besides, I heard him say but the last day, that thou wast no more fit to make a hind, than a serving-man.

PHIL. Sir, you were once my brother.

WILL. True, but that was when you were a son to my father.

PHIL. Ay, and my younger brother: I had then priority of birth

WILL. But now it seems we have got the start of you; for, being but a servant, you are taken a button-hole lower:

PHIL. When will this tedious night give place to day?

WILL. I hope I may command.

PHIL. I must obey.

Enter JOHN *and* SUSAN.

JOHN. My string, Sue! Are these shoes well mundified? Down a your marrowbones, good Sue! I hope you are not so strait-laced but you can stoop. You acknowledge me one of your young masters. If not, 'tis not unknown to you that I know the way to my father.

SUS. Yes, sir; and can tell tales, I know you can; and I have felt the smart on't.

JOHN. Whip me, if you shall not, if you begin once to grow stubborn, why when?

SUS. As humble as your feet. (*Kneels to tie John's shoe.*)

Enter MRS. HARDING.

MRS. H. Why, how now, maid! is this work fitting you? And you sir; you are look'd for in the stable, And should not loiter here. Will you be gone?

PHIL. I am for any service.

(*Exit.*)

SUS. And I too.

(*Exit.*)

MRS. H. We shall find other things for you to do.

WILL. If you cannot, here be they that can. A drudge! a groom! I'll send him of my errands.

JOHN. And if I do not find work for her, I'll do nothing but take tobacco in every room, because, twice a day, I'll make her clean the house.

(*Exeunt.*)

MRS. H. These think, because I am their stepmother,
Their chiefest torture is my most content,
When I protest, to see them thus afflicted,
It grates my very heartstrings every hour.
For tho' before their father's ruthless eye,
And their remorseless brothers, I seem stern,
Yet privately they taste of my best bounty.
And other of my servants are by me
Hir'd to o'ercome their chiefest drudgery.
(*Voices within*). Follow, follow, follow!

Enter YOUNG FORREST *with his weapon drawn.*

YOUNG FOR. I am pursued; and there's no place of refuge
Left to my desperate life. But here's a woman!
Oh, if she harbour soft effeminate pity,
She may redeem me from a shameful death.

MRS. H. A man, thus arm'd, to leap my garden wall!
Help, help!

YOUNG FOR. As you are fair, and should be pitiful;
A woman, therefore, to be mov'd; a Christian,
And therefore one that should be charitable,
Pity a poor distressed gentleman,
Who gives his desp'rate fortune, life, and freedom,
Into your hand.

MRS. H. What are you, sir, that, with your weapon drawn,
Affright me thus?

YOUNG FOR. If you protect my life,
Fair creature, I am a free gentleman;
But if betray me, then a poor man doom'd
Unto a shameful death.

MRS. H. What's your offence,
That such suspicious fear and tim'rous doubt
Waits on your guilty steps?

YOUNG FOR. I've killed a man;
But fairly, as I am a gentleman,
Without all base advantage,
In even trial of both our desp'rate fortunes.
　MRS. H. Fairly?
　YOUNG FOR. And, tho' I say it, valiantly.
　MRS. H. And hand to hand?
　YOUNG FOR. In single opposition.
　MRS. H. In a good quarrel?
　YOUNG FOR. Else let the hope, I have in you of safety,
Turn to my base confusion. Gentle creature,

　　　　　　　　　　(*A cry within, " Follow," &c.*)

I cannot now stand to expostulate,
For, hark! the breath of my pursuers blows
A fearful air upon my flying heel,
And I am almost in their fatal gripe.
Say, will you save me?
　MRS. H. I will. Then climb into that hovel.
　YOUNG FOR. Oh, anywhere.
　MRS. H. Nay, quickly then.
　YOUNG FOR. Your hand, fair lady!
　MRS. H. Away, leave me to answer for you. (*Sits down
to work.*)

　　　　　　　　　　　　　(*Exit* YOUNG FOR.)

　　　Enter OLD HARDING, GOODWIN, FOSTER, *and* OFFICERS.

　OLD HAR. Over my garden-wall! Is't possible?
　GOOD. Over this wall I saw him leap it lightly.
　OLD HAR. That we shall quickly know. See, here's my
　　wife;
She can inform us best.
　FOS. Saw you not, Mrs. Harding, a young man
Mount o'er this garden-wall with his sword drawn?
　MRS. H. My eyes were steadfast on my work in hand,
And, trust me, I saw none.
　OLD HAR. Perhaps he took down to the neighbour village,
And when he saw my wife, alter'd his course.
　MRS. H. 'Tis very like so, for I heard bustling
About that hedge; besides a sudden noise

Of some that swiftly ran towards your fields.
Make haste; 'twas now; he cannot be far off.
    OLD HAR. Gentlemen, take my word: I am High Constable.
It is part of my office: I'll be no shelter
For any man that shall offend the law.
If we surprise him, I will send him bound
To the next Justice. Follow you your search.
    GOOD. Farewell, good Mr. Harding.
    FOS. Your word's sufficient, without further warrant,
Continue our pursuit! All ways are laid;
And ere he reach the city shall be staid.

                          (*Exeunt* GOODWIN *and* FOSTER.)

    OLD HAR. Adieu, good friends.
    MRS. H. Pray, what's the business, sir?
    OLD HAR. Two gentlemen went into the fields to fight,
And one hath slain the other.
    MRS. H. On what quarrel?
    OLD HAR. I had small leisure, to importune that:
Only this much I learnt: the man that's dead
Was great in fault; and he that now survives,
Subject unto the danger of this search,
Bare himself fairly; and his fortune being
To kill a man allied to noblemen,
And greatly friended, is much pitied.
But law must have its course.
    MRS. H. (*aside*) If this be true,
I thank my fate, and bless this happy hour
To save a life within law's griping power.
    OLD HAR. Come, then: the morning's bleak, and sharp the
        air.
Into the fire, my girl; there's wholesome heat,
I'll in, and see my servants set at meat.
    MRS. H. Sir, I'll but end this flow'r, and follow you.
If this should be some bloody murderer,
Great were my guilt to shroud him from the law.
But if a gentleman by fortune crost,
'Tis pity one so valiant and so young
Should be given up into his enemy's hands,
Whilst greatness may perhaps weigh down his cause,

And balance him to death, who thus escaping
May, when he hath by means obtain'd his peace,
Redeem his desp'rate fortunes, and make good
The forfeit made unto the offended law.
Prove as Heav'n shall direct, I'll do my best:
'Tis charity to succour the distrest.

Enter YOUNG FORREST, *above.*

YOUNG FOR.   Fair mistress, are they gone? may I descend?
MRS. H.   No safety lives abroad.   Then, pray, forbear
To speak of 'scaping hence.
YOUNG FOR.   Oh, but I fear!
MRS. H.   My life for yours.
YOUNG FOR.   However poor I fare,
May you of this charitable care
Taste happy fruit.
MRS. H.   You did not kill him foully?
YOUNG FOR.   No, I protest.
MRS. H.   Nor willingly?
YOUNG FOR.   I willingly fought with him, but unwillingly
Did I become his death's man.
MRS. H.   Could you now
Wish him alive again?
YOUNG FOR.   With his hands loose;
And yet he slew my brother.
MRS. H.   Heav'n hath sent this gentleman, because he's
         penitent,
To me for succour: therefore till the violence
Of all his search be past, I'll shroud him here,
And bring you meat and wine to comfort you,
Free, I protest, from all unchaste pretence,
Till by some means I may convey you hence.
YOUNG FOR.   The life you save, if I o'ercome this plunge,
Shall be forever yours: all my endeavours
To your devoted service I will store,
And carefully hoard up.
MRS. H.   Sir, now no more.

                                        (*Exeunt.*)

ACT III.

Enter PHILIP *and* CLOWN.

CLOWN.   Come, good fellow Phil!   What, nothing but
mourning and mowing?   Thy melancholy makes our teams to
vail their fore-tops, and all our jades are crest-fallen; and, (to
see thee wail in woe) in the deep cart-ruts, up to the bellies,
plunge in pain.   My mistress Susan, she's in the same pitiful
pickle too.

PHIL.   Oh, if this hand could execute for her
All that my cruel father hath impos'd,
My toil would seem a pleasure; labour, ease.

CLOWN.   Ease? what's that?   There's little to be found in
our house.   Now we have loosed the plough in the fields,
they'll find work enough about home, to keep us from the
scurvy.   Your hat, Phil! see, here comes our mistress!

Enter MRS. HARDING, *with bread and a bottle.*

MRS. H.   The place is clear: none sees me; now's the time
To bear my sorrowful charge bread, meat, and wine.
These six days I have kept him undiscover'd.
Neither my husband's nor my servants' eyes
Have any way discover'd him.   How now,
Fellows? whither so fast this way?

CLOWN.   Nay, we do not use to go too fast, for falling: our
business at this present time is about a little household service.

MRS. H.   What business have you this way?

CLOWN.   We are going, as they say, to remove, or, according
to the vulgar, to make clean, where Chanticleer, and Dame
Partlet, the hen, have had some doings.

MRS. H.   What dost thou mean by that?

PHIL.   By my master's appointment, I must not say my
father's: he hath commanded us first to make clean this hen-
roost, and after, to remove the hay out of that hay-loft.

Mrs. H. Oh, me! I fear the gentleman's betrayed.
What shift shall I devise?

Clown. By your leave, mistress: pray let's come by you.

Mrs. H. Well! double diligence: your labor has saved:
'Tis done already: Go and take your pleasure.
Son Philip, when I heard my husband speak
Of such a base employment, I straight hir'd
A lab'rer to prevent it, and 'tis done.

Phil. You're kinder, mother, than my father cruel,
And save me many a toil, and tedious travail,
Impos'd on me by your husband.

Mrs. H. O'er this place,
I'll bear a jealous and a watchful eye,
To prevent this discovery. And will you be gone?

Clown. Yes, sweet mistress, if you would but give a wink,
a word, to the dairy-maid for a mess of cream betwixt my
fellow Philip and I: it's good to be doing something; for you
know, my master does not love we should be idle.

Mrs. H. Well, sir, perhaps I shall remember you.

Clown. Come, Phil, let's be gone; and if you chance to
blush at what my mistress hath promised, I'll tell you who
cast milk in your face.

(Exeunt.)

Mrs. H. Shall I compare his present misery
With the misfortunes of this gentleman,
Which might I reckon greater? but I leave them,
And to my charge. We all must yield to fate;
He casts us down that best can raise our state.

Enter Susan, *with something in her apron.*

Sus. Oh, thro' what greater plunges can I pass
Than I have done already? A father's penury —
The good old man dejected and cast down —
My husband even swept from the family
Where he was born, and quite forsook by him
By whom he should be foster'd; made a servant
Amongst his servants, and his brothers' scorn;
These mischiefs make me wish myself unborn.

Mrs. H. Again prevented!

Sus. How hath this meditation drawn my thoughts

From my intended business !   I forgot
What I was sent about.   My master bade me
Scatter this wheat and barley 'mongst the hens ;
And I will soon despatch it.
   MRS. H.   What makes thee
So near the place that I so strictly guard ?
What business have you there ?
   SUS.   Forsooth, my master
Bade me go serve the poultry.
   MRS. H.   Come, you shall nòt ;
For this time I will do it for you.
   SUS.   Mother and mistress too !
'Tis courtesy in you to proffer it,
But should I suffer, you might hold it justly
In me small manners.
   MRS. H.   I say it shall be so.
   SUS.   Shall any servant
Stand still, and see her mistress do her work ?
Pray, pardon me : I should condemn myself
Beyond imagination, should I stand
Idly and see the work done by your hand.
   MRS. H.   I say I will.
   SUS.   My words dare not say nay ;
But my more froward action brooks no stay.   (*Going.*)
   MRS. H.   Then, doubtless, he's betrayed.
   SUS.   Oh, me ! what's here ? why
Here's one that's come to steal your hens, a thief
Who'll filch your poultry.
   MRS. H.   'Tis not so.
   SUS.   Shall I cry thieves aloud ?
   MRS. H.   For heav'n's sake, no !

        YOUNG FORREST *leaps down.*

   YOUNG FOR.   Betray then hapless Forrest.   Once more I lie,
Ordain'd for pity, or prepar'd to die.
What, none but women, and betray me ? then
I see your hearts are flintier far than men.
   MRS. H.   Think not that I'll betray you, nor shall she,
If she respect my love, or her own life.

Sus.   Betray my brother! it shall ne'er be said
I stopt his flight when he had means to 'scape.
    Young For.   Oh, fortune beyond hope! amaz'd I stand
To see my life laid in my sister's hand.
    Sus.   Dear brother!
    Young For.   My sweet sister!
    Mrs. H.   A strange greeting!
And 'twixt two hapless creatures, happy meeting!
    Young For.   What change hath brought you to this down-
cast state?
    Sus.   Nay, what mishap hath ruinated you?
    Mrs. H.   You both forget your dangers: Then leave off
These passive fits, and study for the safety
Of this distressed gentleman, your brother,
Now in the ruthless mercy of the law.
    Young For.   Sister, you've heard my fortunes.
    Sus.   With sad cheer,
Little surmising you had laid so near.
Dear mother, let us crave your farther assistance
In furthering his escape.
    Mrs. H.   I am all yours.
    Young For.   My safety lies in sudden expedition:
Debar me, I am dead.
    Mrs. H.   I have a brother
Lives at Gravesend — an owner and a merchant,
And could we but convey you safe to him,
He soon would ship you over into France.
    Young For.   All ways are laid, and hue and cry sent forth
Thro' ev'ry hundred.   How shall I reach thither
Without discovery?
    Sus.   Here stands an empty trunk in the next room,
Which should be sent by water to Gravesend
To your brother.   What, if we should lock
Him fast in that?
    Mrs. H.   I like it well; but whom
Shall we employ to bear it safe?
    Sus.   Give it my husband and your man in charge:
They two will see it carefully deliver'd.
    Mrs. H.   By them I'll write unto him earnestly
In your behalf, and doubt not of your usage.

YOUNG FOR. The trunk, the trunk! oh, quickly, if you love me.

MRS. H. Come, I'll to write.

SUS. I'll find those that shall bear it.

YOUNG FOR. The plot is likely, but Heav'n knows I fear it.

(*Exeunt.*)

SCENE 2.— OLD HARDING'S *House.*

Enter OLD HARDING, JOHN, *and* WILLIAM.

OLD HAR. Now, boys, no question but you think it long
To have my estate made over to your use.

JOHN. Oh, lord, sir!

OLD HAR. To have your eldest brother quite disabled
Of any challenge of inheritance.

WILL. We think it not long, sir; but if you should use all expedition possible, I should say "Beshrew their hearts that would hinder it." We do not wish our brother disinherited; but if it be your pleasure, Heaven forbid that we, being your sons, should any way contradict it.

JOHN. We should not show ourselves obedient sons, to persuade you to infringe your former vow: for, father, if you remember, you swore long since to do it. And Heaven forbid you should break your oath!

OLD HAR. Boys of mine own free spirit, mine own heart!
And will you see him pine, beg, starve, nay, perish,
Ere you will once relieve him?

WILL. If't be your will, we'll swear to do it.

OLD HAR. And tho' the beggar's brat, his wife, I mean,
Should for the want of lodging, sleep on stalls
Or lodge in stocks or cages, would your charities
Take her to better harbour.

JOHN. Unless to Cold Harbour, where, of twenty chimneys standing, you shall scarce, in a whole winter, see two smoking. We harbour her? Bridewell shall first.

OLD HAR. Lads of my own condition, my own humour!
Call me a scriv'ner: Reach me pen and ink:
I'll do't immediately.

WILL. Run for a scriv'ner, Jack.

JOHN.   Meantime, post thou for pen and ink.

Enter MRS. HARDING, *meeting them.*

MRS. H.   Stay ! no such haste.
Sweet husband, there be fitter times than these
Made choice for such affairs.   There's no enforcement
To make your will, being in such perfect health.
Pray, if you love me, do not talk of death ;
Nor to your safety give such ill presage.
Besides, this expedition in your sons
Shows that they covet more your lands than life.
Defer't then somewhat longer, for my sake.

OLD HAR.   Then, for thy sake, I will.   But, my kind boys,
It is rather to soothe her, than your least wrong ;
I will delay a little, tho' not long.

WILL.   It hath been long a-doing : I would it were once
done.   If he should perk over the perch now, and all fall to our
elder brother, we have used him so doggedly, the least he can
do is to thrust us out of doors by head and shoulders.

JOHN.   Let him alone now : we'll urge him to it at more con-
venient leisure.

OLD HAR.   When heard you from your brother at Graves-
       end ?
Or how falls out his voyage, can you tell ?

MRS. H.   I had a letter from him two days since,
In which he writes me all his goods are shipt,
His wares in hold well stow'd, and nothing wants
Save a fair gale to bring him to the Straits.

OLD HAR.   Heav'n make his voyage prosp'rous ; for thou
       know'st
I have a venture of five hundred pound
Enter'd with him : my fortune joins with his :
If he succeed, it falls out well with me ;
If not, I'm likely to impart his loss.

Enter OLD FORREST.

OLD FOR.   You are well found, sir.

OLD HAR.   Ay ? what art thou, fellow ?

OLD FOR.   You knew me in my pride and flourishing state,
Have you forgot me now ?   As I remember,
We two were bred together, school-fellows,
Boarded together in one master's house,
Both of one form and like degree at school.

OLD HAR.   Oh, thy name's Forrest.

OLD FOR.   Then in those days, your father, Mr. Harding,
Was a good honest farmer, tenant too
Unto my father.   All the wealth he purchased
(Far be upbraiding from me !) came from us,
As your first raiser ; and you call'd me then
Your landlord and young master.   Then was then.
But now the course of Fortune's wheel is turned ;
You climb'd, we fell ; and that inconstant Fate,
That hurl'd us down, hath lift you where we sate.

OLD HAR.   Well, we are lord of all those manors now,
You then possess'd.   Have we not bought them dearly ?
Are they not ours ?

OLD FOR.   I no way can deny it.   I rather come
As a poor suitor to you, to entreat you,
For Heaven's sake and charity's,
To pity my lost daughter, your cast son.
Sir, I in all had but three children left me,
Crutches to bear up my penurious age ;
One of these three was butcher'd cruelly,
His body piteously, alas ! pierc'd thro',
Then had I but two left, my eldest son,
And he's dead, or fled to save his life ;
If he still live, I've wasted, sold, or spent
Ev'n all that little that my fortunes left ;
And now I have but one, one only daughter,
And her I am not able to relieve
With aught save tears and pity.   To these helps,
Oh, lend your fair assistance !   She is yours,
As well as mine.

OLD HAR.   All my part I disclaim,
Both in my son and her.   They crost my pleasure,
And they shall taste the smart.   I was derided.
They that love me shall by my will be guided.

WILL.   And that am I ?

JOHN.   And I, too, father ?

MRS. H.   Base parasites!

OLD HAR.   You ever pleas'd me well ;
And you shall mount the height from which they fell.

Enter PHILIP *and* SUSAN.

OLD FOR.   See, see, alas ! those that sev'n summers since
Saw thy estate, and look upon thee now,
Would at least pity, if not help thy wants.
How happy was thy mother and my wife,
That slept her last sleep long before these sorrows
Did take their birth !

SUS.   Dear father, succour us.
Help to redeem us from this cruel man
That thus insults upon our miseries.

OLD FOR.   Fair daughter, add not to my tedious woes.
Thou bidd'st a blind man guide thee on thy way,
And tak'st a broken staff to be thy stay.

PHIL.   Good sir, release us.

OLD FOR.   It must be then with tears,
For other help I've none ; and they, Heav'n knows,
Can ease but little, but never help your woes.
Sir, if your heart be not of adamant,
Or some hard metal that's impenetrable,
Pity your blood and mine.   So soon grown deaf !
Kind gentlemen ! speak to your ruthless father !
Show yourselves brothers.   Do you turn aside ?
Fair mistress, what say you ?   I see your eyes
In all things with our passions sympathize,
And you are doubtless sprung from gentle blood.
Gentry and baseness in all ages jar;
And poverty and wealth are still at war.

OLD HAR.   Thou grow'st too tedious.   Prithee, friend,
begone!

OLD FOR.   I hope you do not scorn me.

OLD HAR.   The truth is,
I fain would have thee leave me.

OLD FOR.   'Tis no disparagement unto your birth
That you converse with me ?   If I mistake not,
Sure, sure, I am as well born.

OLD HAR.   And yet sure,
'Tis ten to one I shall be better buried.
  OLD FOR.   I am as honest.
  OLD HAR.   Nay, there you are aground.
I'm honester by twenty thousand pound.
  OLD FOR.   Are all such honest, then, that riches have?
  OLD HAR.   Yes, rich and good ; a poor man and a knave.
Away, about thy bus'ness : loiter not
About my gates.   I shall compel thee else.
For thy request, my will is peremptory :
Thy softness makes me much more violent.
Whom thou the more commiserat'st, I contemn.
They're in my deepest hate.   Wife, sons, let's go.

(Exeunt.)

  OLD FOR.   With eyes in tears sunk, heart circumvolv'd in
woe.
  SUS.   What shall we now do ?
  PHIL.   What, but endure the worst ?
When comfort's banished, welcome all extremes !
Yet I have sent my fellow, or my man,
To prove some friends to help to stock a farm.
I have not yet their answer !   'Tis the last
Of all our hopes.   That failing, we have run
Our latest course, outcast, and quite undone.

(Exeunt.)

SCENE 3.— *The* MERCHANT'S *house.*

Enter the MERCHANT, *reading a letter, and after him* YOUNG FORREST.

  MERCH.   My sister writes how your occasions stand,
And how you are to use my secrecy
In a strange business that concerns your life.
She hath left nothing unremember'd here,
Or slightly urg'd, to make me provident
And careful of your safety.   Gentle sir,
Tho' I am a stranger to your fortunes,
Yet for her sake whose love I tender dearly,
I am all yours ; my house to entertain you ;
My purse to furnish you in any course ;
My ship, if you'll to sea, is at your service ;

Make choice in which of these, in all, or any,
You will employ my faithful industry.

YOUNG FOR. Oh, sir, your unexpected courtesy
To a poor stranger challenges the name
Of brother to the kindest gentlewoman
That ever breath'd this air. You cannot chuse
But be of one strain, that such kindness use.
You bade me to make choice of all your favours.
My poverty and my necessity
Do both of them, in my extremes, conserve
To make me think the mean'st of any means,
That can unplunge me from this gulf of trouble,
To be much better than I can deserve,
To be much greater than I dare desire,
Being too poor to merit, too dejected
To aim at any hopes.

MERCH. You wrong your worth.
You have desert sufficient, that she writes
In your behalf; and I commend her for it.
Methinks I see such honest parts in you,
That upon weaker urgence than these lines
I would build much affection on these gifts,
Which I see nature hath endowed you with.
Indeed I flatter not. None flatter those
They do not mean to gain by. 'Tis the guise
Of sycophants, such great men to adore
By whom they mean to rise, disdain the poor.
My object is much otherwise intended ;
I fain would lose by him whom I commended.

YOUNG FOR. If ever thus my weak ability
Grows strong again, I will employ it solely
To shun the base sin of ingratitude
Tow'rds you and your fair sister.

MERCH. Will you use me ?

YOUNG FOR. But what shall I return you in exchange
Of those great favours ?

MERCH. Come, your love, your love.
'Tis more than all I can attempt for you
Amounts unto. Pray let me know the most
Of my employment.

YOUNG FOR.   Then will you but provide me a safe waftage
Over to France, to Flanders, or to Spain,
Or any foreign coast.   I dare not trust
My native country with my forfeit life.
Sir, this is all I would entreat of you.

MERCH.   You're modest in your suit.   The more you use me,
The more I think you love me.   Therefore
This night I'll get you waftage o'er to France.
Such sea-apparel as I use myself
You shall accept part.   Here's ten pounds in gold,
And wheresoever you shall live hereafter,
Pray let me once a year receive from you
Some brief or note.   I'll not return your love
Idle or empty-handed.

YOUNG FOR.   My life's yours,
And lesser satisfaction than my life
Is much too little.

MERCH.   Much too much.   No more,
No more, I do entreat you.   I am now
Upon a voyage to the Straits myself.
But 'twill be two days hence.

YOUNG FOR.   Heav'n be your guide!
As I find you, so find friends in your need!
Blushing I run into your countless debt
More sums of love than all my hoard can pay.
But if these black adventures I survive,
Ev'n till this mortal body be ingraved,
You shall be lord of that which you have saved.

MERCH.   Only your love.   Come, we'll provide this night
For your safe waftage, and your secret flight.

(*Exeunt.*)

SCENE 4.—*A Street.*

Enter CLOWN, FOSTER, GOODWIN, *and a* GENTLEMAN.

FOS.   Speak with us?   Why, what's the business?

CLOWN.   Nay, that's more than I can resolve you upon the
sudden.   It may be there's some great fortune fallen to him of
late, and he would impart the benefit to you.

GOOD. Nay, then, let's go. Where shall we find him?

CLOWN. A word to the wise. It may be that he's in some monstrous extreme necessity, and would gladly borrow some money of you, or so.

GOOD. Ay, said'st thou so? now I remember me, I needs must home. I have some business? I'll see him at some other time.

CLOWN. Nay, but one word more.

FOS. We cannot stay now.

GENT. Not I: a great occasion calls me hence.

CLOWN. Nay, then, I see you are apt to take a man at the worst still. If you knew what little need he hath to borrow: "Borrow?" quoth he, "a good jest." You know he and I, my fellow Phil and I, 'mongst other works that my master uses to put us to, we use to dig and delve: now, if we have found a pot of money, and would trust you with the laying of it out, why so!

FOS. How!

CLOWN. Marry, even so. You know his father is such a dogged old curmudgeon, he dares not for his ears acquaint him with it.

GENT. Prithee, go on.

CLOWN. 'Twere kindness in him to choose you out of all the friends he hath in the world to impart this benefit to, were't not? and say true.

GENT. Troth, he was always a kind, honest youth, and would it lay in me to pleasure him!

GOOD. In troth, or me! he should command my purse and credit both.

FOS. Where might speak with him?

CLOWN. Hard by, sir, hard by. But stay, gentlemen, suppose there is no such matter as finding of money; but what we missed in digging, to supply his present necessities, he hopes to find from you! I promise you, I partly doubt such a matter.

FOS. How! I forgot myself; I needs must home.

GOOD. Troth, nor can I stay.

GENT. In sooth, nor I. (*Going.*)

Enter PHILIP, *meeting them.*

PHIL. Gentlemen, whither so fast? I sent to speak with you.

CLOWN. I can assure you, sir, they are better to speak withal, than to borrow money of. One word or two with you, my friends (by your leave, master). Gentlemen, I love you well ; and that you may know I love you, I would make bold to reveal a secret to you. My young master here, though you see him in these homely accoutrements, simple as you stand here, he has more to take to than I'll speak of. He might, ay, marry might he, he might go brave and shine in pearl and gold : he hath now on his instant possession a thousand pound thick.

FOS. A thousand pounds ?

CLOWN. Nay, old lads, he hath learnt his 1-2-3-4 and 5. And never cost him ten shillings.

GOOD. Five thousand pounds ?

CLOWN. You know where you hear it. Mum ! here's your tale and talesman.

GENT. Good, good, proceed.

CLOWN. Now lift up your large ears and listen. To whom should he reveal all this wealth but to some friend ? and how should he know a friend but by trying of him ? and how should he try a friend but by troubling of him ? and how should he trouble a friend but by borrowing money of him. Now, gentlemen, it may be at first, he'll make his case poor and pitiful to you.

FOS. Only to try us ?

CLOWN. Only to try you : have you no brains ? do you think we have need of money ? has any of you occasion to use a hundred pound ? need of money ! as I said afore, so I say again, only to try you. He has done the like to four or five that I know. Now, because they would not pity his supposed poverty, he would not acquaint them with this infinite mass of wealth. You have brains, wits, apprehension. If he makes his case known to you, lay it on. If I said lay it on, lay it on. You are not everybody. If I had not seen some sparks in you, you had not been the men. Lay it on !

FOS. Enough, enough ; I understand thee fully ;
Kind Master Philip, will you use my aid
In any fair employment ?

GOOD. Sir, or mine ?

GENT. Or mine ?

PHIL. Worthy friends ! even one as all !

Freely to speak, as you are gentlemen,
And I have from childhood have protested love,
As you are Christians, therefore to the poor,
Such as I am, should be most charitable,
Help with your plenty to relieve my wants.
You know my labour, and have seen my need.
Then take some pity of my poor estate,
And help to ransom me from slavery,
By lending me some money.

    CLOWN.   Did I not tell you so? lay it on.
    Fos.   Sir, you shall have a hundred pound of me.
    GOOD.   What need you use him, and myself so near?
    GENT.   Trouble not them, sir; you shall ha't of me.
    CLOWN.   Take it, master; take it all.
    PHIL.   Oh, heav'ns! where slept this friendship all this while?
Who said that charity was fled to heaven,
And had no known abiding here on earth?
See, these that knew me disinherited,
And to have no means to supply my wants,
Strive who should most engage his purse and credit,
To one so much oppress'd with poverty!

    CLOWN.   Alas! sir, you see their kindness.
(*To the rest*) I told you how strange he would make it.
Lay it on.

    Fos.   Pray, sir, accept my kindness.
    GOOD. }
    GENT. } Pray take mine.
    CLOWN.   Pray, master, take their courtesies.
    PHIL.   I'll use them all,
And only borrow twenty pounds a-piece
To stock a poor farm for my wife and me.
Some threescore pounds will do it.

    CLOWN.   Now, now, lay it on.
    GENT.   Take it all of me.
    GOOD.   Why all of you sir? is not mine as ready?
    Fos.   When one can do't, what need you trouble three?
But for the thousand pound, sir; do not think,
But you may trust me with the whole employment
Of all such moneys, and never trouble these.

    PHIL.   What thousand pound?

Good. Tho' it be six thousand,
I durst be steward of so great a sum.
    Clown. Why, master fellow Phil!
    Phil. Do you mock me, gentlemen?
My wealth amounts not to a thousand straws.
    Clown. I told you he would make it strange. Lay it on.
    Fos. Make not your wealth so dainty; for we know
You have at least six thousand pound in bank.
You may impart it unto us your friends.
    Phil. Who hath deluded you, derided me,
And made a mockery of my poor estate?
Now I protest I have not in the world
More riches than these garments on my back.
    Good. Impossible; why, here's my tale, and my talesman.
    Clown. No, sir, you are deceived. Here is your tale, and
you yourself are your talesman; for you carry it about with
you. The truth is, gentlemen, that we have betwixt us both
no more crosses than you see.
    Phil. Only the late hope of those sixty pounds,
Promised by you unurg'd and uncompell'd,
May raise my ruin'd fortunes.
    Gent. Will *you* disburse it all, that were so forward?
    Fos. I have no money. Do it you for me.
    Good. It is but one man's labour, do't yourself.
If you have none, I have less. God be with you. One stays
for me at home.
    Gent. Nay, take me with you, sir.
    Phil. Why, gentlemen! will you revolt your words?
    Fos. I have no money.
    Phil. But now you strived which man should lend me most.
    Fos. But then we reckon'd, sir, without our host.
Then we suppos'd you rich, but being grown poor,
I've made a foolish vow to lend no more.
                                                            (*Exit.*)

    Gent. I have made the like. You know your father
        threatens
To disinherit you, and should we lend,
You, being poor, should of our purses spend.
                                                            (*Exit.*)
    Phil. Tho' I be poor, Heav'n may enable me.

Good. Heav'n may do much. That's all the beggar's saying.
Let me hoard wealth. You seek for wealth by praying.

(*Exit.*)

Phil. The time may come ere long, so I divine,
To punish those that at their power repine.

Enter a Pursuivant, *meeting the* Clown.

Purs. Whither away so fast, sirrah? In the Queen's name,
I command you stay.

Clown. What are you that look so big?

Purs. A pursuivant.

Clown. If you be so pursy, can you lend us any money? I
assure you, it was the last business we were about. Or else,
tell me the reason you stay my passage.

Purs. Sirrah, I have a Proclamation to publish, and because
myself am something hoarse, and thou hast a large wide mouth,
and a laudable voice, I charge thee, for the better understanding of the multitude, to speak after me, word by word.

Clown. If it be nothing else, do but advance me, and I'll
speak high enough. Come now and teach me my new lesson.

Purs. "Whereas two famous Rovers on the Sea."

Clown. Whereas two famous Rogues upon the Sea.

Purs. "Purser and Clinton."

Clown. That lost their purses at the Clink.

Purs. "Long since proclaimed pirates."

Clown. Long since proclaimed spirits.

Purs. "Notwithstanding Her Majesty's commission."

Clown. Notwithstanding Her Majesty's condition.

Purs. "Still keep out."

Clown. And will not come in.

Purs. "And have of late spoiled a ship of Exeter."

Clown. And have of late spoiled all the sheep in the
Exchequer.

Purs. "And thrown the chief merchant overboard."

Clown. And thrown the merchant's cheeses overboard.

Purs. "I, therefore, in Her Majesty's name."

Clown. I, therefore, in the name of Her Majesty.

Purs. "Proclaim to him or them."

Clown. Proclaim to them or him.

PURS. "That can bring in these pirates' ships or heads."

CLOWN. That can bring in these piecrusts or sheeps'-heads.

PURS. "A thousand pound sterling."

CLOWN. A thousand stares and starlings.

PURS. "If a banished man, his country."

CLOWN. If a man, he shall be banish'd his country.

PURS. "If a condemned man, liberty."

CLOWN. If a man at liberty, condemned.

PURS. "Besides her Majesty's especial favour."

CLOWN. Besides her Majesty's spectacles and favour.

PURS. "And so God save the Queen."

CLOWN. And have you done now, sir?

PURS. I have. Farewell!

(*Exit.*)

CLOWN. Farewell, Mr. Pursuivant: he hath so filled my head with proclamations.

(*Exit.*)

ACT IV.

SCENE I.—*On board of Ship. A great alarum, and shot.*

Enter PURSER *and* CLINTON, *with* MARINERS, *bringing in the* MERCHANT, *bound prisoner, with others.*

PURS. Now, valiant mates, you have maintain'd this fight
With courage, and with wonted hardiment.
The spoil of this rich ship we will divide
In equal shares; and not the mean'st of any
But by the custom of the sea may challenge,
According to his place, rights in the spoil.
Tho' outlaws, we keep laws amongst ourselves:
Else we could have no certain government.

CLIN. A gallant prize, and bravely purchas'd too,
With loss of blood on both sides. A sea-fight
Was never better manag'd, nor exploited
With more exchange of hostile opposition.
We did not look for such a valiant spirit
In any merchant's breast; nor did we think

A ship of such small burthen, so weak mann'd,
Would have endur'd so hot and proud a fight.

MERCH.   Nor did I think the Providence of Heaven
Would so have flavoured men of base condition,
Such as profess wrong, piracy, and theft,
Have spoiled my men, and ransack'd every corner
Of my surprised bark ; seiz'd all my substance,
And shared amongst you my best merchandise ;
And not alone undone me, and in me
All that are mine, but in o'erwhelming us,
Shook the estate of all my creditors.

PURS.   What's that to us ? men of our known condition
Must cast behind our backs all such respects.
We left our consciences upon the land,
When we began to rob upon the sea.

CLIN.   We know we're pirates, and profess to rob ;
And would'st not have us freely use our trade ?
If thou and thine be quite undone by us,
We made by thee ; impute it to thy fortune,
And not to any injury in us ;
For he that's born to be a beggar, know,
Howe'er he toils and trafficks, must die so.

MERCH.   If you must needs profess this thriving trade,
Yet since the seas afford such choice of store,
You might, methinks, have spar'd your countrymen.

PURS.   Nay, since our country have proclaim'd us pirates,
And cut us off from any claim on England,
We'll be no longer now call'd Englishmen.

MERCH.   Clinton, I know thee, and have us'd thy skill,
Ere now in a good vessel of my own,
Before thou took'st this desp'rate course of life.
Perhaps if now thou dost me a good office,
Time may enable me to quit thy love.

CLIN.   Troth, I could wish we had light of any other ;
But since thy fate hath cast thee upon us,
We must neglect no opportunity.
For they that intermit advantages,
Must know Occasion's head is bald behind.
My merry mates, come top your cans apace,
Pile up your chests with prizes to the lids,

And stuff the vast hold of our empty ship
With such rich wares as this our prize affords.
Supply your biscuits with such choice of wines,
As freely come, brought by th' auspicious winds,
T'unlade themselves and seek for stowage here;
Since wine comes freely, let's make spare of beer.

PURS.   Let cans of wine pass round in healths thro' all.
Such golden prizes come not ev'ry day;
Nor can we always meet such choice of spoils.
First, bind the Merchant; lay him fast in hold,
And, having seiz'd all his best merchandise,
Pierce with your ordnance thro' his ship's craz'd keel,
And sink her down into the deep abyss,
Whence not all the cranes in Europe or the world
Can weigh her out again.

CLIN.   Let it be so,
Lest she prove prize unto a second foe.

MERCH.   Be't as my fate shall please.   My loss I value
But as goods lent me, now to be paid back.
But that which most afflicts my sorrowful soul
Is that my friends have ventur'd largely with me,
Especially my sister, who I fear
Will brook that ill which I with patience bear.

PURS.   Place him below the hatches as our prisoner;
And now to part our purchase, bravely won,
Ev'n with the hazard of our dearest lives.

CLIN.   The danger past still makes the purchase sweet.
Come, first drink round, my merry mates; that done,
Divide in peace what we by war have won.

(*Exeunt.*)

SCENE 2.— *On board a Privateer.*

Enter YOUNG FORREST, *like a Captain of a Ship, with* SAILORS *and*
MARINERS, *entering with a flourish.*

YOUNG FOR.   Gentlemen, and my merry mates at sea,
Those special favours you have crown'd me with
Can never be deserved upon my part,
So weak is my ability and knowledge

In navigation and exploits at sea.
Yet since your loves so far exceed my worth,
That, of an unexperienc'd gentleman,
You have preferr'd me above many other
To be your captain and command your ship,
I hope to bear myself so even and upright
In this my charge, that it shall not repent you
Of the least honour to my grace decreed.

    1ST MAR. Our captain being lately slain in fight,
We by your valour 'scap'd our enemies,
And made their ship our prize. Since we first knew you,
All our attempts succeeded prosperously,
And Heav'n hath better blest us for your sake.

    2 MAR. When first we took you to our fellowship,
We had a poor bark of some fifteen ton,
And that was all our riches. But since then
We have took many a rich prize from Spain,
And got a gallant vessel stoutly mann'd,
And well provided of ordnance and small shot,
Of men and ammunition, that we now
Dare cope with any carrack that does trade
For Spain.

    YOUNG FOR. We dare do anything that stands with justice,
Our country's honour and the reputation
Of our own names. But amongst all our spoils,
I wonder we have 'scaped the valiant pirates,
That are so much renown'd upon the sea.
That were a conquest worth the hazarding.
Besides a thousand pounds' reward propos'd
To that adventurer that can bring them in,
My peace and pardon, tho' a man condemn'd,
Is by the proclamation ratified.

    1ST MAR. The ocean scarce can bear their outrages,
They are so violent, confounding all,
And sparing none, not their own countrymen.
We could not do our country greater service,
Than, in their pursuit, to engage our lives.

    YOUNG FOR. Ay, could we meet those Rovers on the Sea,
So famous for their piracies and thefts,
So fear'd of all that trade for merchandise,

So proud of their strong vessels, and stout ging,
That man her with their proud artillery,
That thunders wrack to every ship alike;
Oh, with what ardour and inflam'd desire
Would we in the mid sea encounter them.
Climb to the main-top, boy. See what you ken there!

    Boy. I shall, I shall, sir.

    Young For. We seek for purchase, but we tak't from foes,
And such is held amongst us lawful spoil.
But such as are our friends and countrymen
We succour with the best supply we have
Of victuals or munition, being distrest.

    Boy (*above*). Ho there!

    1st Mar. Eh, boy?

    Boy. A sail.

    1st Mar. Whence is she?

    Boy. That I cannot ken. She appears to me out of our
hemisphere; no bigger than a crow.

    Young For. Descry her better.
Oh, that it were the desp'rate pirate's ship,
On that condition we might grapple straight,
And try our desp'rate fortunes on ev'n change!
But I that have been born to misery
Can never be so happy. Oh, my fate!
When shall I pass away this tedious night?
Or when, my stars, will you burn out more bright?

    Boy. Boatswain, ho!

    1st Mar. Whence comes thy ken?

    Boy. She makes from south to west.

    2 Mar. How bears she?

    Boy. To the leeward.

    Young For. Clap on more sail, and quickly fetch her up.
What colours bears her main-top?

    Boy. She's not so near in ken.

    Young For. Discover her more amply. Now my mates,
Prepare yourselves; for it may be some prize.
You, master Gunner, load your ordnance well,
And look well to your cartridges and fire:
See that your gunner-room be clear and free,
Your matches bear good coals, your priming powder

Pounded, not dank. Next charge your murderers
For fear of boarding. Steersman, port the helm,
And bear up towards them. Be they friends or foes,
We'll hail them, if Heav'n please. And, Master, you
Heed well your compass. Boatswain, with your whistle
Command the sailors to the upper deck,
To know their quarters, and to hear their charge.

    BOY. Captain, ho!

    YOUNG FOR. The news? Whence is her flag?

    BOY. She bears the cross of England and St. George.

    YOUNG FOR. Then she's a friend for England; and St.
      George
Our gallant vessel in her main top bears,
And all our preparations needless then.

    BOY. Arm, rather; for I see them from afar
Make all provision for a present fight:
They've managed their hatches, hung their pendants out, dis-
played their ensigns, up with all their fights; their matches in
their cocks; their smoking linstocks are likewise fired within
their gunner's hands; and hark! they shoot already.

                        (A shot heard.)

    YOUNG FOR. Come, descend.
The pirate! Fortune, thou art then my friend!
Now, valiant friends and soldiers, man the deck,
Draw up your fights, and lace your drablers on;
Whilst I myself make good the forecastle,
And ply my musket in the front of death.
Quarter yourselves in order, some abaft,
Some in the ship's waist, all in martial order.
Our spritsail, topsail, and topgallant sail,
Our mainsail, bolt-sprit, and our mizen too,
Are hung with waving pendants; and the colours
Of England and St. George fly in the stern.
We fight against the foe we all desire.
Alarum, trumpets! gunner, straight give fire!

                           (Exeunt.)

SCENE 3.— *On board the Pirate-vessel.*

Enter PURSER *and* CLINTON, *with their* MARINERS, *all furnished with sea-devices fitting for a fight.*

CLIN. Give them a full broadside. Oh, Mr. Gunner, your upper tier of ordnance shot over. You gave not one shot between wind and water, in all this skirmish.

GUN. Sir, you speak not well. I pierced them with my chace-piece through and through. Part of their capstring too I, with a piece abaft, shot overboard.

PURS. Oh! 'twas a gallant shot! I saw it shatter some of their limbs pieces. Shall we grapple, and lay their ship abroad? where be these irons to hook them fast?

CLIN. I fear they are too well manned ;
For see the gunner, ready to give fire
Unto their murderers, if we stay to board them.
Shall we set sail and leave them?

PURS. How can we, when our ship has sprung a leak !
Being ready now to founder in the sea?
Some ply the pump. Oh, for one lucky bullet,
To take their mainmast off! He that can make it
Shall have a treble share in this next prize.

GUN. I shall go near it from my lower tier.

CLIN. Gunner, do that: 'tis all that we desire.

(*Exeunt.*)

SCENE 4.— *On board the Privateer.*

Enter YOUNG FORREST *and his* MARINERS.

1ST MAR. Where is the gunner, captain ?

YOUNG FOR. Where he should not be. At his pray'rs, I
    think.
Is this a time to pray, when the sea's mouth
Seems to spit fire, and the billows burn ?
Come, hand with me, and we will board the pirates
Instantly.

1ST MAR. Hoist up more sails and fetch 'em roundly up,
And with their gallant vessel grapple straight.

YOUNG FOR.   I spy the pirates in the very prow
And forehead of their ship, both wafting us
With their bright swords.   Now, steersman, take thy turn ;
And boatswain, with your baser trumpet's sound
Mingle your whistle's shrill.   Oh, 'tis a music
The mermaids love !
   1ST MAR.   Who hates it, that's a soldier?
   2D MAR.   Thy linstock, gunner ! take thy level right :
The wind is ours to help us in the fight.
   YOUNG FOR.   It blows a stiff gale.   It makes all for us :
Ev'ry commander once more to his charge !
He that this day shall die, dies honourably :
The cannon's basilisks and ordinance
Shall toll his fun'ral peal ; and some, now sound,
Shall die three deaths in one, shot, burnt, and drown'd.
Come, spare no powder till you see our ship,
Whose hard, tough ribs, hew'd from the heart of oak,
Now black with pitch, be painted blue with smoke.

                                                    (*Exeunt.*)

SCENE 5.—*On board the Pirate Ship.   A great alarum and
                    flourish.*

Enter YOUNG FORREST *and his mates, with* PURSER *and* CLINTON, *with
                    their* MARINERS, *prisoners.*

   YOUNG FOR.   First, thanks to Heav'n for this great victory,
Bought with the fearful hazard of our lives,
And large expense of blood on either part.
   PURS.   We now are captives that made others thrall.
Thus ebbs may flow, and highest tides may fall.
   CLIN.   The latest day must come to have his date :
Stars govern all, and none can change his fate.
   YOUNG FOR.   Such pris'ners, as these pirates keep in hold,
Release them straight.   The riches of their ship
We 'mongst you will divide in equal shares ;
To ev'ry man's desert, estate, and place.
   PURS.   Fortune, I put defiance in thy face !
Thy best we've tasted, and thy worst we know.
We can but pay what we to Nature owe.

Enter the MERCHANT, *brought in with other* PRISONERS.

MERCH. Surpris'd again! whose pris'ner am I now?
I'm Fortune's ball. Whither am I bandied?
Having lost all before, is't possible
That I can now be made a second prize?
I lost my wealth in my first hostile strife;
And nothing now is left me save my life.

YOUNG FOR. These pris'ners we will, at our further leisure,
Peruse, and know their fortunes and estates.

MERCH. That captain I should know. That face of his
Is with mine eye familiar. Sure 'tis he
Whose life, I, by my sister's means preserved,
With money and apparel furnish'd him,
And got him place at sea; and hath he now
Forgot me? What, not know me? The world right!
When rich we honour, being poor we spight.
Ne'er look so strange. I do not mean to claim
Acquaintance of such men as are ingrate.
All my good deeds, once done, I throw behind,
Whose meed in heav'n, not earth, I look to find.

YOUNG FOR. That merchant I have known; and now I
        better
Survey him, 'tis the man to whom I owe
All that I have, my fortunes, nay, my life.
What reason have you, sir, to fly me so?
Since unto you, and to your brother's wife,
My hopes, my power, my whole estate is due,
From whom my means and all my fortunes grew.

MERCH. Do you know me, then?

YOUNG FOR. Think you I can forget,
Or slightly cancel such a countless debt?
Behold my ship, my conquest, and my prize,
These pris'ners, with my full command, is yours;
Yours, only yours: they at your service rest:
Alas! dear friend, how came you thus distrest?

MERCH. These pirates robb'd me, and have seized my goods,
With which they've stuffed their hold. My brother's venture
With mine own substance they have made their spoil.

YOUNG FOR. All which, behold, re-deliver you,
And to the utmost farthing will restore.
Besides, I make you partner in our prize,

And herein am I only fortunate
To prove a grateful debtor.

MERCH.   Your gratitude exceeds all courtesy,
Both of my sister's party and my own.

YOUNG FOR.   It comes much short of either.   Oh, dear sir,
Should I forget your friendship, show'd in want,
And done in my extremest poverty,
It were a sin, of heav'n unpardonable.
This pirate's ship, load with your merchandise,
You shall straight man for England where arriv'd,
Commend me to the mirror of her sex,
Your sister, in the humblest phrase you can,
To whom deliver, as from me, this jewel,
The best our voyage yields.   Tell her, from me,
That gentleman, whose innocent life she saved,
Hath, by that token, her remembrance crav'd.
To my brother and my sister, this small sum,
To buy their service from their father's hand,
And free them from his slavish servitude.

MERCH.   I shall do all you will; and thus o'erswayed,
Needs must report your debts are doubly paid.

YOUNG FOR.   Having my pardon purchased, and my
   pris'ners
Deliver'd to the sentence of the law,
My next affairs shall be to visit her.

PURS.   Our case is otherwise.   Our next affairs
Is to betake us to our beads and prayers.

CLIN.   Be as be may, base Fortune I defy;
We bravely liv'd; and I'll as boldly die.

YOUNG FOR.   Hoist sail for England, with our long-wished
   prize,
Whilst we applaud that Fortune he defies.

                                        (*Exeunt.*)

ACT. V.

Scene i.— Old Harding's *House.*

Enter Old Harding, Mrs. Harding, Foster, Goodwin, William, John, Philip, *and* Susan, *the two last setting forth a table.*

Old Har. You are welcome, gentlemen. Come take your
places,
As your degrees are. Wife, the chair is yours.
My loving boys, sit. Let the servants wait.

John. Brother, that's you.

Old Har. This day I do entreat you, gentlemen,
After the table's ended, to be witness
Unto some deeds that must inherit these,
And him that is my eldest quite disable ;
To which I must entreat your friendly hands.

Fos. Mine is still at your service.

Good. So is mine, sir.

Will. Oh, day long-look'd for !

John. Now shall we live like two young emperors. Oh,
day worthy to be writ in the almanac in red letters, for a most
famous holiday !

Phil. Well, jest on, gentlemen : when all is tried,
I hope my patience will exceed your pride.

Will. Wait at my elbow with a clean trencher, Phil. Do
your duty, and have your due. You know your place. Be
ready with a glass of beer, and when I say fill, fill.

Enter the Clown.

Clown. If please your worship, here is a manner or a kind
of some fowl desires to have some conference with you.

Old Har. A sea-fowl !

Clown. Yes, a sea-gull. I mean a mariner. He says he
hath some news to tell you from my mistress her brother at
sea.

Old Har. Touching my venture. Prithee, guide him in.

Clown. He smells, as they say, of pitch and tar. If you
will have him to perfume the room with his sea-musk, I'll shew
him the way instantly.

OLD HAR. I prithee do, and that with expedition.

MRS. H. I did not look thus soon to hear from him.

OLD HAR. I fear some strange mishap hath late befall'n him.

Enter SAILOR *and* CLOWN.

MRS. H. Now, honest friend, the news! How fares my
brother?

OLD HARD. How doth my venture prosper?

SAIL. Sir, your ship is taken, all your goods by pirates
seiz'd,

Your brother pris'ner, and of all your venture

There's not the value of one penny saved.

OLD HARD. That news hath pierc'd my soul, and enter'd me

Quite through the heart: I'm on the sudden sick,

Sick of (I fear) a mortal malady. Oh, oh!

JOHN. How is it with my father?

OLD HARD. Worse and worse.

The news of such a great and weighty loss

Kills all my vitals in me.

WILL. Father! for Heaven's sake, father, die not yet, before
you have made over your land.

JOHN. That were a jest, indeed! why, father, father!

OLD HARD. Trouble me not. If I survive this night,

You two shall be my heirs.

WILL. This night, if it be thy will.

MRS. H. Alas, how fare you, sir?

JOHN. Take courage, father.

OLD HARD. Son, lead me hence, and bear me to my bed,

My strength doth fail; I cannot help myself.

WILL. Run, run for the writings. They are ready drawn at
the scrivener's. Bid him bring them quickly, with a vengeance.

OLD HARD. Let them alone. My hand hath not the strength

To guide my pen. Let them alone, I say.

Support me to my bed; and, my kind neighbours,

Assist me with your pray'rs; for, I divine,

My soul this night shall amongst the angels shine.

JOHN. Marry, Heaven forbid! Can he find no time to die
but now?

Let's in; and haunt his ghost about the writings.

(*Exeunt.*)

Manent GOODWIN *and* FOSTER.

Fos. 'Tis strange the bare report of such a loss
Should strike a man so deeply to the heart!

Good. I oft have read the like. How some have died
With sudden joy, some with exceeding grief.

Fos. If he should die intestate, all the land
Falls to the elder brother; and the younger
Have nothing, save mere from his courtesy.

Good. I know it, neither lands nor movables.
Come, let us hear what further news within.

Enter the CLOWN.

CLOWN. O, my master, my master! what shall I do for my
poor master? the kind churl has departed! never did poor
hard-hearted wretch pass out of the world so like a lamb! alas!
for my poor, usuring, extortioning master! many an old widow
hast thou turned into the street, and many an orphan made
beg their bread! Oh, my sweet, cruel, kind, pitiless, loving,
hard-hearted master. He's dead; he's dead; he's gone; he's
fled; and now full low must lie his head! Oh, my sweet, vile,
kind, flinty, mild, uncharitable master!

Fos. Dead on the sudden? 'tis exceeding strange!
Yet for the eldest son it happens well.

Good. Ill for the younger brother.

Enter WILLIAM *and* JOHN.

WILL. Jack!

JOHN. Will!

WILL. The land's gone.

JOHN. Father's dead.

WILL. We have made a fair hand on't, have we not? who
shall fill the glass now? and wait upon the trenchers?

JOHN. Nay, who must go to plough, and make clean the
hen-roost, rub horse-heels, lead the wains, remove the billets,
cleanse the shoes: and, indeed, who must do all the drudgery
about the house?

WILL. Could he find no time to die but now? I could even
cry for anger. Here they come!

Enter PHILIP *and* SUSAN, *well habited, the former with bags of money,*
MRS. HARDING *and others.*

PHIL.   My father's dead.

MRS. H.   Alas! for my dear husband!

PHIL.   Comfort yourself; altho' he die intestate,
It shall not hurt you.   We have found you kind,
And shall be now as willing to requite you,
As able.   How now, brothers! do you weep?
And bear a part with us in heaviness?
No, no; your griefs and ours are contrary.
I grieve I've lost a father; she a husband.
This doth not move you; you lamenting stand,
Not for a father's loss, but loss of land.
Do you remember with what rude despite,
What base contempt, and slavish contumely,
You have despis'd me and my dear-loved wife?

JOHN.   We partly remember it.

PHIL.   So do not I.
I have forgot it quite.   In sign whereof,
Though had you got my lands, Heav'n knows how ill
You would have dealt with me, thus I'll use you.
Receive your patrimony.   (*Gives them the bags.*)

CLOWN.   No more fellow Phil now; but here receive your
proportions!

PHIL.   Your diet if you please is at my table,
Or where you please, if you refuse my kindness.

WILL.   Kindness unlooked for! thanks, gentle brother.

JOHN.   Why, this gold will never be spent.

CLOWN.   Oh, it is an easy thing to bring this mountain to a
mole-hill.

JOHN.   This is more of your courtesy, than our deserving.
To trouble your table, being so many ordinaries in town were
somewhat superfluous.

PHIL.   Spend but in compass.   Rioting eschew.
Waste not, but seek t'increase, your patrimony.
Beware of dice and women.   Company
With men of best desert and quality.
Lay but these words into your hearts enroll'd;
You'll find them better than these bags of gold.

WILL.   Thanks for your coin and counsel.   Come, Jack, this
shall be lavished among the suburbs.   Here's drink money
dice-money, and drab-money.   Here's money by the back, and

money by the belly. Here's that shall make us merry in claret,
muskadine, and sherry. Farewell, brother!

JOHN. My most bounteous brother.

(*Exeunt.*)

CLOWN. Farewell, young masters.

PHIL. (*to* GOOD. *and* FOS.) And now my vile friends, such
as fawn on plenty!
And cannot bear the very name of want!

CLOWN. We have found the mine now.

PHIL. You that disabled once the power of Heaven,
And scorned my state, unable to be rais'd!

CLOWN. You see, here's your tale and your talesman.

PHIL. Take heed, lest here, for your unthankfulness,
That which once rais'd do not remove your estates.
God be with you! henceforth, howe'er you speed,
Trust not riches and despise not need.

CLOWN. One threescore pound will do it.

(*Exeunt* GOODWIN *and* FOSTER.)

PHIL. Mother, the thirds of all my father's lands
Are yours, with whatsoever you like else.
And now, sweet Sue! it glads me I shall make thee
Partner of all this plenty, that bor'st part
With me in all extreme necessities.

SUS. You're all my wealth ; nor can I taste of want,
Whilst I keep you. O, would these fortunes raise
My downcast father, or repeal my brother,
My banish'd brother, to his native home,
I were in all my thoughts at peace with Heaven!

PHIL. All that I have is theirs. My only sorrow,
Next to my father, is in part for them,
And next for your dear brother (*to* MRS. HARDING) ta'en at sea,
Whose loss, if he survive, we will repair,
Ev'n with the best of our ability.
But come unto our father's burial first,
Whom, though his life brought sorrow, death content,
We cannot but with funeral tears lament.

CLOWN. And now no fellows, unless it be at foot-ball.

(*Exeunt* PHIL., SUSAN *and* CLOWN.)

MRS. H. Heaven being just, could not deal longer roughly

With one so virtuous and completely honest.
He merits all he hath.   But to my state:
I am at once doubly unfortunate:
I have lost a husband and a brother, too.

Enter MERCHANT.

MERCH.   A husband, sister, but no brother.   Lo!
That brother lives.
MRS. H.   And can it, heaven, be so?
MERCH.   You are the cause I live.
MRS. H.   I, brother? how?
Tidings were brought into this place but now
Your ship was spoil'd — you pris'ner.
MERCH.   And 'twas true:
Yet, all these losses I regain'd by you.
MRS. H.   By me?
MERCH.   By you.   And, sister, thus it was:
You sav'd the life of a young gentleman,
Whom for your sake I furnish'd out to sea.
He, when my ship was taken, I surpris'd,
And bound, and cast in hold, restor'd my fortunes,
And, besides, all my merchandise restored,
Wherein you bare chief venture, made me sharer
Of the rich pirates' prize.
MRS. H.   That gentleman?
MERCH.   The self same, in whose life, you
Did save yourself some thousand pounds, I have,
As further token of his gratitude,
In this choice jewel he commends to you
Millions of gratulations and kind thanks,
Besides unto his sister store of gold,
To redeem her wretched husband and herself
From my deceased brother's slavery,
Which now I see pale death hath done for them.
MRS. H.   You speak of unexpected novelties,
With which we will acquaint their sorrowful souls.
These tokens will be joyful to them both,
And tidings of his safety welcomer
Than that great sum by him regain'd at sea.

MERCH. We do them wrong to keep news of such joy
So long from them, which we'll no longer smother.
Two thousand pounds I bring you, and a brother.

(Exeunt.)

SCENE 2.— *Near Execution Dock.*

Enter the SHERIFFS; *the* MARSHAL *of the Admiralty, with the silver oar;*
PURSER *and* CLINTON, *going to execution.*

PURS. Now, how is it with thee, Clinton ?
CLIN. Well, well.
PURS. But was't not better when we reigned as lords,
Nay, kings, at sea ? the ocean was our realm ;
And the light billows in the which we sail'd
Our hundreds, nay, our shires, and provinces,
That brought us annual profit. Those were days.
CLIN. Yes, golden days ; but now our last night's come,
And we must sleep in darkness.
PURS. Worthy mate,
We have a flash left of some half-hour long,
That let us burn out bravely ; not behind us
Leave a black, noisome snuff of cowardice
In the nostrils of our noble countrymen.
Let's die no base example.
CLIN. Thinks Tom Watton,
Whom storms could never move nor tempests daunt,
Rocks terrify, nor swallowing gulfs affright,
To whom the base abyss in roughest rage
Shew'd like a pleasant garden in a calm,
And the sea-monsters but like beasts at land
Of profit or pleasure, Clinton can be affrighted
With a halter ? Hemp him strangle that thinks of him
So basely !
PURS. In that word thou hast put a second sentence
Of our lives. Yet, Clinton, never wast my thoughts of thee.
Oh, the naval triumphs thou and I have seen,
Nay, ourselves made, when on the seas at once
have been as many bonfires, as in towns
Kindled upon a night of jubilee ;

As many ordnance thund'ring in the clouds
As at kings' coronations; and dead bodies
Heav'd from the hatches, and cast overboard,
As fast and thick as in some common pest,
When the plague sweeps cities.

CLIN.   That it had swept us then, too!   So the seas
Had been to us a glorious monument,
Where now the fates have cast us on the shelf,
To hang 'twixt air and water.

SHER.   Gentlemen,
Your limited hour draws nigh.

PURS.   Ay, that's the plague we spoke of; yet no greater
Than some before have tasted; and hereafter
Many be bound to suffer; and if Purser
(As dying men do seldom deem amiss)
Presage not wrong, how many gallant spirits,
Equal with us in fame, shall this gulf swallow,
And make this silver oar to blush in blood!
How many captains that have aw'd the seas,
Shall fall on this unfortunate piece of land!
Some that commanded islands; some to whom
The Indian mines paid tribute, the Turk vail'd!
But when we that have quak'd, nay, troubled floods,
And made armadoes fly before our stream,
Shall founder thus, be split and lost,
Then be it no impeachment to their fame,
Since Purser and bold Clinton did the same!

CLIN.   What, is our ship well tackled?   We may launch
Upon this desp'rate voyage?

HANG.   Corded bravely.

PURS.   Call up the boatswain!   Soundly lash the slave
With a rope's end.   Have him unto the chest,
Or duck him at the main-yard.

HANG.   Have me to the chest?   I must first have you to
the gallows.   And for ducking, I am afraid I shall see you
ducked and draked too.

PURS.   Oh, you brave navigators, that have seen,
Or ever had yourselves, command aboard,
That knew our empire there, and our fall now,
Pity at least us that are made the scorn
Of a base common hangman!

SHER. Thou dost ill to offend them at their deaths.

HANG. I have, and long to make an end of them.

PURS. Hadst thou but two months since wrinkled a brow,
Look'd but askew, much less unloos'd thy lips
To speak — Speak, said I ? nay, but lodg'd a thought
Or murmur of the least affront to us,
Thee, basest of all worms'-meat, I had made
Unwholesome food for haddocks! But I ha' done.

CLIN. Enough, Tom Watton, with these sheets, not sails,
A stiff gale blows to split us on yon rock.

PURS. And set sail from the fatal Marshal seas, and Wapping is our harbour, a quicksand that shall swallow many a brave marine-soldier, of whose valour, experience, skill and naval discipline, (*being lost*) I wish this land may never have need! But what star must we sail by? or what compass?

HANG. I know not the star: but here's your compass. (*Shewing the rope.*)

PURS. Yes, that way points the needle. That way we steer a sad course, plague of the pilot! Hear you, Mr. Sheriff! you see we wear good clothes: they are paid for and our own. Then give us leave our own amongst our friends to distribute. There's sir, for you. (*Gives coat and hat to his followers.*)

CLIN. And you. (*Does the like.*)

PURS. The workman that made them took never measure on a hangman's back. Wear them for our sakes, and remember us. There's some content for him, too. (*Gives money to the* HANGMAN.)

HANG. Thank your worships.

CLIN. I would your knaveship had our worship's place,
If hanging now be held so worshipful.

PURS. But now our sun is setting: night comes on.
The wat'ry wilderness o'er which we reigned
Proves in our ruins peaceful. Merchants trade
Fearless abroad as in the river's mouth,
And free as in a harbour. Then, Fair Thames,
Queen of fresh water, famous thro' the world,
And not the least thro' us, whose double tides
Must overflow our bodies; and, being dead,
May thy clear waves our scandals wash away,
But keep our valours living! Now, lead on.—

Clinton! thus arm in arm, let's march to death;
And, wheresoe'er our names are memoriz'd,
The world report two valiant pirates fell,
Shot betwixt wind and water. So farewell!

(Exeunt in procession.)

SCENE 3.— OLD HARDING'S *House.*

Enter OLD FORREST *and* YOUNG FORREST.

OLD FOR. A father's blessing, more than all thy honours,
Crown thee, and make thy fortunes growing still!
Oh, Heav'ns! I shall be too importunate
To ask more earthly favours at your hands,
Now that you, after all these miseries,
Have still reserv'd my son safe and unscorn'd.
Besides thy pardon and thy country's freedom,
What favours hath her grace conferr'd on thee?

YOUNG FOR. More than my pardon and the meed propos'd,
To grace the rest, she styl'd me with the Order
Of Knighthood; and, for the service of my country,
With promise of employments of more weight.
The pirates were committed to the Marshalsea,
Condemned already, and this day to die.
And now, as part of my neglected duty,
It rests I visit that fair gentlewoman
To whom I stand indebted for my life.
That necessary duty once performed,
Out of my present fortunes to distribute
Some present comports to my sister's wants.

OLD FOR. A grateful friend thou art, a kind, dear brother,
And a most loving son.

Enter MRS. HARDING, PHILIP, SUSAN, *and* MERCHANT.

PHILIP. Sir, more than all these fortunes now befall'n me,
A fate midst all disaster unexpected,
My noble brother's late success at sea
Hath fill'd me with a surplusage of joy.
Nor am I least of all endear'd to you,
To be the first reporter.

MERCH.   'Tis most true ;
And I the man that in the most distress
Had first share of his bounty.

MRS. H.   Of his goodness
We have had sufficient taste already ;
But to be made more happy in his sight
Would plenally rejoice us.

SUS.   It would prove
Like surfeit after sweetmeats.

YOUNG FOR.   See all my friends ; but first let me salute
Her to whom I am most bound.

SUS.   My most dear father !

OLD FOR.   My blessing, meeting with a husband's love,
Make thy years long and happy !

MRS. H. (*to* YOUNG FOR.)   You are most grateful,
And much beyond my merit.

SUS.   O, spare me, sir !
To fly into his arms that hath so long
Fled from me !

YOUNG FOR.   My sweet sister !

PHIL.   Bar me not all the blest fruition
Of what in part you've tasted.   Sir, I am one
Amongst the rest that love you.

YOUNG FOR.   I take't, my sister's husband ! unto me
Therefore one most intir'd.

MERCH.   Sir, the same ;
And I, tho' last in my acknowledgment,
Yet first in due arrearage.

YOUNG FOR.   You I know
To be a worthy merchant, and my friend,
To whose, next to your sister's, courtesy
I stand engag'd most for a forfeit life.
But him, next to the Pow'rs divine above,
I ever must adore.   And now, fair creature,
I dare more boldly look upon the face
Of your good man than when I saw you last.

MERCH.   And that's some question.

YOUNG FOR.   Wherefore hath that word
Struck you with sudden sadness ?

MRS. H.   My husband !

PHIL.   He's late dead, and yet hath left her
None of the poorest widows.

YOUNG FOR.   Dead, did you say?
And I a bachelor? now on whom better
Or justlier can I confer myself
Than to be hers by whom I have my being,
And live to her that freely gave me life?
There is a providence that prompts me to't,
And I will give it motion.   Gentle lady,
By you I am, and what I am by you
Be then to me, as I have styl'd you last,
A Lady.   Heav'ns have made you my preserver,
To preserve me for yourself; losing a husband,
Who knows but you have sav'd me to that end,
That lost name to recover? and by me
Sweet interchange and double gratitude?
I left you sped, but find you now despoil'd,
Married, you ventur'd for my single life,
Widow'd, by me to gain the name of wife.

MERCH.   What, pause at the motion?   You are not
My sister, if you deny him.

PHIL.   Let me plead for him.

SUS.   O, doubly link me to you! be you styl'd
My brother and my father.

OLD FOR.   Will you let my age join, and make me proud
To say that, in my last days, barren of issue,
I have got so fair a daughter.

YOUNG FOR.   Sweet, your answer?

MRS. H.   Sir, I should much mistake my own fair ends,
Should I alone withstand so many friends.
I am yours, and only so.

YOUNG FOR.   I yours the same;
And, Lady, now I kiss you by that name.

Enter CLOWN.

CLOWN.   What, kissing already! then I smell another wedding towards; and in no fitter time than now.   Prepare yourselves, gentlemen and gentlewomen.   Make a hall! for I come
to present you with a mask.

PHIL. What mask?

CLOWN. Not such as ladies wear upon their faces, to keep the foul from the fair; but a plain mask, or rather more properly I may call it a mumming, because the presenters have scarce a word to speak for themselves.

PHIL. If there be any that appear as friends,
And come to grace our feast in courtesy,
Admit 'em, prithee.

CLOWN. That shall I, sir, and with all expedition,
And that without drum, without fife, or musician.

Enter WILLIAM, JOHN, GOODWIN, *and* FOSTER.

These two lines shall serve for the prologue. Now enter, Scena prima — Dramatis personæ. These be the actors. Yet let me entreat you not to condemn them before you hear them speak.

PHIL. Amazement startles me. Are these my brothers?

CLOWN. By the father's side, it would seem; for you know he was a hard man; and, it should seem, 'tis but a hard world with them.

PHIL. And these my false friends, that distrusted Heaven, and put their faith in riches? I pray gentlemen, How comes this change?

JOHN. How comes this change, say you? no change of pastures, which they say makes fat calves, but change of drink, change of women, change of ordinaries, change of gaming, and one wench in the change — all these help'd to make this change in us.

WILL. And change is no robbery. I have been robbed, but not at ruff; yet they that have robbed, you see, what a poor stock they have left me. A whore stole away my maidhead, ill company my good conditions; a broker robbed me of my apparel; drink of my wits; and dice of my money.

PHIL. This is no more than expectation.
But how come *you* thus alter'd? (*To* GOODWIN *and* FOSTER.)

CLOWN. If you had said halter'd, sir, you had gone more roundly to the business.

FOS. Sir, there was coining laid to my charge, for which (tho' I acquit myself) I made my estate over unto a friend, (for so I thought him) but now he has cozen'd me and turned me out of all.

GOOD. In dead of night my counting-house was broke ope by thieves, and all my coin (which was my whole estate and the god I then did trust in) stole away; I left a forlorn beggar.

PHIL. Oh, wondrous, why, this passes!

CLOWN. It may pass among the rest for a scurvy jest; but never like Mother Pass's ale; for that was knighted.

MERCH. Ale knighted? how, I prithee?

CLOWN. You have heard of ale-knights: therefore it is not improbable that ale may be knighted.

MERCH. Thy reason.

CLOWN. Why, there is ale in the town that passes from man to man, from lip to lip, and from nose to nose. But Mother Pass's double ale, I assure you, sir, sir-passes; therefore knighted.

PHIL. Leave trifling; for more serious is the object
Offer'd before our eyes. In these, Heav'n's justice;
In these a most remarkable precedent
To teach within our height to know ourselves.
Of which I make this use. You are my brothers,
(A name you once disdain'd to call me by)
Your wants shall be reliev'd. You that distrusted
Heav'n's providence, and made a mock of want
And other's misery, no more deride!
Part of your loss shall be by me supplied,
According to my power.

YOUNG FOR. My noble brother!
You teach us virtue; of which I could wish
All those that see good days make happy use.
So those distress'd; for both there's precedent.
But to our present nuptials. Reverend father!
Dear Lady! Sister! Friend! Nay, Brothers too!
But you, sir (*to Philip*), most conjoinéd and endear'd!
In us, the world may see our fate well scanned:
Fortune in me by Sea, in you by Land.

(*Exeunt omnes.*)

FINIS.